Sweet Valley
HIGH.

Double Love

Sweet Valley
HIGH®

Double Love

Secrets

Sweet Valley
HIGH ®

Double Love

WRITTEN BY **KATE WILLIAM**

CREATED BY
FRANCINE PASCAL

LAUREL-LEAF BOOKS

Published by Laurel-Leaf
an imprint of Random House Children's Books
a division of Random House, Inc.
New York

Originally produced by Cloverdale Press.
Originally published by Bantam Books, New York, in 1983.

Visit us on the Web! www.randomhouse.com/teens

Educators and librarians, for a variety of teaching tools, visit us at
www.randomhouse.com/teachers

Library of Congress Cataloging-in-Publication Data
William, Kate.
    Double love / written by Kate William ; created by Francine Pascal. — 1st
Laurel-Leaf ed.
        p. cm. — (Sweet Valley High)
    Summary: Jessica connives to steal Todd Wilkins, Sweet Valley High's
star basketball player, away from her twin sister Elizabeth.
    ISBN 978-0-440-42262-4 (pbk.)
    [1. Twins–Fiction. 2. High schools–Fiction. 3. Schools–Fiction.] I. Pascal,
Francine. II. Title.
PZ7.W65549Do 2008
[Fic]–dc22

2007021040

RL: 6.0
April 2008
Printed in the United States of America
10 9 8 7 6 5 4 3 2 1
First Laurel-Leaf Edition

CHAPTER 1

"OKAY, WHEN DID I get so hideous?" Jessica Wakefield groaned. She leaned in toward her bedroom mirror as her twin sister, Elizabeth, rolled her eyes. "Seriously, Liz, it's like somebody snuck into my room last night and whacked me with the ugly stick."

"Yeah. That happened," Elizabeth said, digging through a pile of clothes on Jessica's bed.

"I'm totally serious!" Jessica protested. "First of all, I gained, like, five pounds since last week—all in my hips and butt," she said, turning around and craning her neck to see her rear view in the mirror. Her perfect-size-four rear view. "And I hate my hair. I mean, that new shampoo I bought did none of the things it was supposed to do. I'm all split ends and frizz."

"Uh-huh," Liz said disinterestedly.

"Plus I've got a zit! A huge one! Look at this thing, Liz! It's the zit that ate Sweet Valley!"

Jessica got right up in her sister's face.

"You're right, Jess," Liz said flatly. "You're completely deformed. You should definitely stay home from school today."

Jessica's face crumpled and she collapsed face-first on her unmade bed. "You suck."

"What? I'm just agreeing with you."

"Fine. Just leave me here to rot. I'm not fit for normal society."

Elizabeth laughed and pulled her sister back up, maneuvering her in front of the mirror, where they stood side by side. With their shoulder-length blond hair, blue-green eyes, and perfect California tans, Elizabeth and Jessica were exact duplicates of one another, down to the tiny dimples in their left cheeks when they smiled. Each wore a gold lavaliere around her neck—matching presents from their parents on their sixteenth birthday last June. The only way anyone who didn't know them very well could tell them apart was by the tiny beauty mark on Elizabeth's right shoulder. Those who *did* know them well knew that Elizabeth's style was more sophisticated and preppy, while Jessica's was up-to-the-minute trendy. Plus Elizabeth always wore a watch, while Jessica did not. Time was never a problem for Jessica. She always felt that things didn't really start until she arrived.

"Look at me," Elizabeth said to her twin, who did as she was told. "Now look at you." Jessica did. "If you're hideous, then I'm hideous too. Are you calling me hideous?"

Jessica's brow knitted. "You're a freak, you know that?"

"Yeah. A freak who can't find her new white sweater," Elizabeth said, returning to her search. "Where did you say you put it?"

Jessica hadn't said. Because she'd worn it without asking and spilled marinara sauce down the front, then forgotten to wash it right away. The stain had set, and now the sweater was ruined beyond all hope. She was just opening her mouth to plead ignorance when the phone rang.

"I got it!" she cried, grabbing the phone from her bedside table. "Hello?"

She took the phone out into the hallway to avoid her sister's growing impatience. Why didn't the girl just give up already and wear something else? Liz could be so stubborn sometimes.

"Hey, Liz? Or is this Jessica?" a boy's voice asked.

"It's Jessica," she replied. Hmmm. A call from a guy before the first school bell had rung. Her day was looking up already.

"Oh, hey, Jess. It's Todd."

Todd Wilkins? Even better. Todd was one of the most coveted guys in school. Tall, dark, and yum.

"Hey. What's up?" she asked, leaning back against the wall with a smile. Jessica had never really considered Todd before, but hey, if he was calling her, maybe he deserved a spare thought. Or two.

"Not much. Is Liz there?" he asked.

Instantly, the smile was gone. He was calling for Liz? The star wide receiver of the football team, captain of the basketball team, a shoo-in for best-looking and most popular, was calling for her brainiac sister? What was this, some kind of reality-show prank?

"Actually, she's kind of busy right now," Jessica said, taking a few steps away from her bedroom. "Spell-checking her latest marathon paper, of course. Such a nerd.

So, how's the team? I saw that insane catch you made at practice the other day. ESPN highlight reel all the way."

Get him talking about himself, Jessica thought. *Guys love that.*

"You saw that?" The blush was evident in Todd's voice. Jessica glowed with triumph.

"Are you kidding? I practically missed my dismount because of it," Jessica told him. "Didn't you hear me cheering? I stopped practice and everything." It also couldn't hurt to remind him that she was captain of the cheerleading squad that went all out to support him every week.

"Thanks. That's . . . uh . . . thanks," Todd stammered.

"Can't wait for the first game," Jessica said happily. She just loved to make guys nervous. "I bet you'll have college scouts coming out for you in no time."

"I don't know about that, but thanks," Todd said humbly.

Jessica smiled. Sometimes she was so good she could hardly believe it herself. Two seconds of flattery and the guy had forgotten all about Liz. Boys were so predictable.

"Anyway, do you think you could see if Liz is free yet?" he asked.

Jessica frowned. Okay, maybe not *totally* predictable. "Oh, you know what? She just got in the shower."

"I could wait," Todd said hopefully.

Jessica forced a laugh. "Are you kidding? She'll be in there forever. Liz takes the longest showers." Big lie. Jessica was actually the hot-water hog of the family. In fact, Elizabeth usually had to take short showers because the hot water stopped half a minute in, thanks to Jessica.

Todd took a deep breath. "All right, then. I guess I'll just . . . talk to her later. Could you tell her I called?"

"No problem!" Jessica said. "See you in school!"

"Yeah. See ya."

Jessica hung up the phone and rolled her eyes. Todd Wilkins calling for Liz? What a joke. Elizabeth probably didn't even know Todd existed. She was way too serious for a gorgeous athlete like him.

"Who was that?" Elizabeth asked when Jessica traipsed back into her room. She had two neatly folded piles of Jessica's clothes in front of her now—clothes that had been strewn all over the room five minutes ago.

"Todd Wilkins," Jessica replied, tossing the phone onto her bed. "I don't know why he didn't call my cell. I'm sure he has the number."

Elizabeth paused midfold. "Todd called you?"

"Yeah. Guess he just couldn't wait another half hour to talk to me in school," Jessica said with a shrug, turning toward her reflection again.

"Oh." Elizabeth attacked another mountain of clothes, tearing through them like a tornado.

"Liz? What's wrong?" Jessica asked, staring at her sister in the mirror. She was whipping clothes at the bed as if they'd somehow offended her.

"What's wrong is I wish you'd stop taking my stuff without asking," Elizabeth blurted out.

Jessica rolled her eyes as she turned around. "So borrow something of mine if you want. I have white sweaters too, you know."

"That's not the point," Elizabeth said, irritated.

"Then what is the point?" Jessica asked.

"The point is . . . ," Elizabeth said, looking around at the mess. "The point is . . ." Finally, her shoulders slumped. She took a deep breath and sighed. "Just forget it. I'll wear something else."

She turned and walked out of Jessica's room, stepping over a pile of stuff on the way out the door. Jessica shook her head at her sister's back as she went. Liz really was way too possessive of her things.

Todd Wilkins. Huh, Jessica thought. *We would look pretty hot together.*

With one last fluff of her hair and a quick, appreciative glance at her reflection—hideousness forgotten—Jessica grabbed her books and headed downstairs for breakfast. There was nothing that put her in a good mood faster than the thought of a brand-new conquest.

CHAPTER
2

ELIZABETH WAKEFIELD LOVED her life. She really did. But sometimes it felt just a tiny bit unfair. Like this morning, for example. All she'd wanted to do was take a nice, long shower, slip into her new white sweater, and go to school happily anticipating a possible conversation with Todd Wilkins.

Instead, she'd taken a short shower, abbreviated by a blast of cold water because Jessica had used up all the hot. Then she'd gone into her third drawer for her white sweater only to find that Jessica had "borrowed" it. And then the guy she'd been crushing on ever since the beginning of the year had called for, once again, Jessica. What next? Was Jess going to eat all the French toast before Liz even got downstairs?

Taking a deep breath, Elizabeth clipped her hair back from her face and stared at herself in the mirror.

It's fine. Everything's fine, she thought. *It was just one phone call. It doesn't mean anything.*

But why would Todd be calling Jessica? Over the last couple of weeks, things had been happening between Liz and Todd. There was that time in the cafeteria when their eyes had met across the table and he had held her gaze for that long, incredible moment before smiling his heart-stopping smile. Then there was that flirtatious conversation after chem class last Friday. Liz had really thought Todd was starting to like her back. Was that all just her hopeful imagination? Was he really interested in—please, no—Jessica?

And even worse, was Jessica into him too?

Elizabeth sighed and swept some clear lip gloss across her lips. She hadn't told her sister about her crush on Todd because she knew Jessica would mock her endlessly for it. Todd was not Elizabeth's usual type. He was a jock, for one, and Elizabeth usually went for more cerebral guys. Plus he was part of the popular crowd—the crowd

Jessica was at the center of but Elizabeth always avoided, worried that their marathon conversations about clothes and makeup and cheerleading would rot her brain. Todd, of course, was anything but shallow, though Elizabeth knew that if she confessed her feelings for him, she would never live it down. And now she was beyond happy that she'd made the decision to keep it to herself.

Todd and Jessica. It makes perfect sense, Liz thought. The star of the football team *would* go for the the captain of the cheerleading squad. It was practically a law.

"Liz! Your breakfast is getting cold!" Alice Wakefield called up the stairs.

"Coming, Mom!" Liz replied.

She grabbed her messenger bag, gave herself one last, bolstering look, and went downstairs to join her family. Her mother handed her a plateful of French toast and fresh fruit as she walked into the room.

"Morning, sweetie," Mrs. Wakefield said, tucking her blond hair—the same shade as Liz's—behind her ear.

"There's the sunshine," her father joked. Ned Wakefield looked up from the newspaper and passed Liz the OJ as she sat down.

"Hi, guys," Elizabeth replied, pulling the front section of the paper toward her.

Jessica had already wolfed down half her breakfast and was staring at some miniskirts in the Style section.

"So, girls, looks like your father and I are both going to be working late tonight," Mrs. Wakefield said, sipping her coffee. "I've got that design for the new downtown restaurant to finish, and your dad's working on a case."

"Big one," Mr. Wakefield said, his brown eyes sparkling. "Huge."

"What's up, Dad? A merger? A war between two giant conglomerates?" Jessica asked.

"Close," he said. "But there's three sides to this one." He lowered his paper for a second to look at his daughters. "Actually, it may interest the two of you. It has to do with the Sweet Valley High football field."

"Gladiator Field, Dad," Jessica corrected him, as if her father were just so ignorant.

"Really?" Elizabeth asked, intrigued. "What's going on?"

"Unfortunately, as a lawyer on the case, I can't say more than that just yet," Mr. Wakefield replied. "Marianna and I are working on it, though, so don't worry. Besides, I *will* be late again. Isn't that enough bad news for you?"

"Okay, mystery man," Jessica joked.

"Wait, Mom, if you're both working late does that mean we're walking home from school today?" Elizabeth asked. "Because if we are I should probably change my shoes. . . ."

"Nope. No walking. Your dad picked up the Jeep from the shop last night, so you girls officially have wheels again," her mother replied.

"We do? Thank you! Thank you! Thank you!" Jessica cried, jumping up and throwing her arms around her father.

Elizabeth laughed. Their red Jeep Wrangler had been in the shop for less than a week, and Jessica acted as if they had been tortured to within an inch of their lives.

"I'm glad you're so excited, Jess, but don't forget you're grounded from driving for three weeks," her father said. "Liz is going to be the keeper of the keys."

Jessica's smile instantly dropped. "What? This is so unfair!"

"Jessica, we've already been through this," Mrs. Wakefield said sternly. "You're the one who had the accident. You've got to learn some responsibility."

"I said I was *sorry*," Jessica protested, slumping down in her chair again. "Three weeks? Why don't you just tell me I can never drive again?"

Elizabeth smirked as her parents exchanged amused smiles. Jessica had a serious talent for exaggeration.

"Well, you should have thought of that before you drove your car into a mailbox," Mr. Wakefield said.

"Whatever," Jessica replied grumpily.

"We should probably go. It's getting late." Elizabeth got up and took the keys her mother held out for her.

"Yeah. And with Grandma Liz driving it's gonna take an hour for us to get there," Jessica added. She grabbed her bag and traipsed out of the kitchen without so much as a backward glance.

"Have a good day, you guys," Elizabeth said to her parents.

"You too, sweetie," her mother replied.

Then Liz joined her sister, who was drumming her fingers impatiently on the front doorjamb.

"Come on, drama queen," Elizabeth said, walking by her. "If you're good I'll let you pick the CD."

"Oh, ha ha," Jessica replied, slamming the door behind them. "God, this morning sucks."

You have no idea, Jess, Elizabeth thought. *Not a clue.*

• • •

"Accident," Jessica muttered as Elizabeth drove through the quaint downtown area of Sweet Valley. "It was just a tiny dent. She makes it sound like a six-car pileup on the freeway."

"That *tiny dent* cost a fortune to fix," Elizabeth said dryly, wishing her sister would stop complaining and let her enjoy the drive through the valley. Liz loved the green jewel of a California town that was their home. She loved the gently rolling hills, the palm trees swaying in the breeze, and the soft white-sand beach only fifteen minutes away. Going over the hill toward school, she could see the sun glinting against the blue waters of the Pacific in the distance. She took a deep, soothing breath and let her crappy morning fade away.

"Don't you wish we lived up here on the hill like Lila and Bruce?" Jessica asked, gazing out the window at the sprawling mansions.

"No. I like our house," Elizabeth replied. "And we just got a pool. Isn't that enough for you?"

"Yeah, I guess," Jessica grumbled.

"Dad worked his butt off on that oil company case to get the bonus that paid for it, and he's been working late every night since," Elizabeth said. "You could try being grateful."

"I am grateful! Sheesh. De-clench already," Jessica said. She glanced at Elizabeth, then turned slightly in her seat. "Actually, I've been kind of wondering about that. Aren't you a little freaked about Dad?"

"What? Why?" Liz asked.

"Because! You know he's not alone when he's working late, Liz. He's with that woman all the time."

"You mean Ms. West?"

"Yeah. *Her*. But you heard what Dad called her this morning," Jessica said. *"Marianna."*

Elizabeth felt a thump of foreboding. She'd been wondering about her dad's odd hours lately too, but Jessica's noticing them meant the situation must be really glaring. Jessica rarely noticed anything that didn't directly affect her social life.

"Well, that *is* her name," Elizabeth said lightly, hoping to make them both feel better.

"A *sexy* name. And she has a sexy voice, too. She picked up the phone the other day when I called his office and it was like, whoa. She sounds like one of those phone-sex chicks."

"Jessica!" Elizabeth admonished her.

"I'm just saying!" Jessica replied. She sighed and looked out at the spacious homes. "Anyway, I never said I don't like our house. But Lila Fowler is, like, rolling in green. I would kill to be as rich as her for even one day."

"Okay, fine. But what about all the stuff that comes with it?" Liz asked.

"You mean the great clothes and the servants waiting on you hand and foot? I could handle that."

"No. I mean the psycho feud," Liz replied. "Bruce Patman's parents wanting every rock in Sweet Valley to stay exactly where it's been for seventy-five years and the Fowlers wanting to build over everything in sight. Their families are constantly bad-mouthing each other on TV and in the papers, and Lila and Bruce can't even look at each other. It's ridiculous."

"Small price to pay for Paris couture, Liz," Jessica said. Sweet Valley High came into view as the Jeep crested a small hill, and Jessica sat forward in her seat. "Okay. We're here. Stop and let me drive into the parking lot."

"What?" Liz said, slapping Jessica's hand away from the wheel. "You're insane. You heard what Mom and Dad said."

"You heard what Mom and Dad said." Jessica mimicked her twin nastily.

Elizabeth sighed. "Jessica—"

"Elizabeth," Jess mimicked her again. "What's the big deal? It's like two blocks! Just let me drive!"

"There's no good place to pull over," Elizabeth protested. "It's not like Mom's dropping you off at the front door. I'm driving our car."

"Yeah, like that's any better," Jessica said. "Great. Now it's too late. Thanks a lot, Liz."

Elizabeth clenched her teeth and pulled the Jeep into an empty space in the student parking lot. She looked at her sister, who was staring straight ahead, stone-faced and annoyed. "It's only three weeks. It'll pass like that," she said encouragingly.

"You know, sometimes having a goody-goody for a sister really sucks," Jessica spat.

She got out of the car and slammed the door so hard Elizabeth winced. Somehow it always turned out this way. Elizabeth just did what her parents asked of her, and she always ended up feeling guilty. It was so unfair.

"Jessica, calm down," Elizabeth said, getting out of the car to face her stormy-eyed twin. "I'll talk to them for you. Maybe they'll let you drive tomorrow."

"Tomorrow!" Jessica sneered. "You may be a tomorrow person, Liz, but I am a today person. Don't do me any favors." She crossed her arms over her chest and turned her head, staring obstinately away.

Elizabeth took a deep breath. There was no talking to

Jessica when she got in this mood. Luckily, at that moment, she spotted the perfect excuse to bail—her best friend, Enid Rollins, waving her down from the lawn.

"Jess, I have to go," Elizabeth said. "Enid wanted to talk to me before homeroom."

"Oh, Eeny Rollins needs you? Fine. Go ahead. Go talk to the biggest blah in school," Jessica said. "Wait, on second thought, don't. Someone might think it's *me* talking to her."

"What is your problem with Enid?" Elizabeth asked. "If you'd just hang out with us once, you'd see how cool she is."

"Cool? Are you kidding me? She's a total geek, Liz," Jessica replied with a scoff. "Plus there's something freaky about her," she added, looking toward Enid and shuddering dramatically.

"Freaky?" Elizabeth laughed. "Like what?"

"Like—" Jessica glanced past Elizabeth's shoulder and the irritated line that had formed above her nose disappeared. "Like nothing. Forget I said anything," she said quickly. "I'm sorry." She gave Elizabeth a quick and powerful hug, nearly lifting her off the ground. "You go talk to Enid. I'll see you at lunch."

"Okay. What's your deal, Ms. Mood Swing?" Elizabeth asked.

"Nothing," Jessica said with a blithe shrug. "I just don't like to hold a grudge."

Yeah, right, Elizabeth thought. When they were little, Jessica had once given their older brother, Steven, the silent treatment for six months because he'd cheated at a game of Monopoly. But Liz wasn't about to stick around and question her twin. She'd been given a free pass out of the standoff. She'd be an idiot not to take it.

"Okay, then. See you later," she said. She turned and jogged across the parking lot to join Enid at the edge of the grass.

"Hey, Liz!" Enid said brightly.

"Hey! So what's the big news?" Elizabeth asked.

"Shh! Not so loud," Enid replied, looking around as though the entire student body were listening.

"Uh, there's nobody here," Elizabeth pointed out.

"Oh. Right." Enid laughed, flashing her pretty smile. She lifted her long brown hair over her shoulder and blushed, looking down at the ground. "Let's sit."

"Okay."

Liz sat on the curb with her friend and waited while Enid collected herself. No matter what Jessica said, Enid was not a geek. She might have been quiet when Elizabeth had first starting hanging out with her in creative writing class last year, but once Liz got to know her,

Enid had turned out to be very smart and very funny. But Liz thought there was something almost mysterious about her friend, as though she knew things other people didn't. And she found that intriguing. Jessica, however, had written the girl off after one meeting, just because she hadn't been cracking up at every one of Jessica's jokes and enthralled by her stories about her many crushes.

"Okay, you can't tell anyone what I'm about to tell you," Enid said.

Elizabeth's heart skipped a beat. "Who is he?"

"What?" Enid's green eyes widened.

"You like someone! It's totally obvious. Who is it?"

"Okay, you should totally go on *Oprah*," Enid said, blushing. "How do you read people like that?"

"It's a special talent," Liz joked with a shrug.

A few yards away, Bruce Patman's sleek black Cadillac XLR Roadster convertible pulled into an empty parking space. Elizabeth shook her head as a group of freshmen girls paused to drool.

"Well, you're never going to guess who called me," Enid said. "Ronnie Edwards! That new guy in history class? He's friends with Caroline Pearce."

"The guy no one has ever heard speak?" Elizabeth asked.

"Well, I have," Enid replied, giggling. "I saw him looking at me in the cafeteria the other day, and then he asked for my notes after class because he zoned out. Which, we both know, is easy to do in Ms. Markey's class."

"Definitely," Liz replied. Even she, straight-A student that she was, sometimes had trouble with Markey's infamous monotone.

"Well, then he called me to ask some questions about the notes, and we ended up talking for hours, and then . . ."

"Then what?" Elizabeth asked.

"Then he asked me to the Harvest Dance!" Enid announced.

"No way!"

"Way!" Enid replied.

"That's incredible, Enid!"

"I know! I'm so psyched," Enid said, her feet bouncing up and down. "So, has *he* asked you yet?"

Elizabeth's heart took a sudden drop. "Oh, um . . . no."

Enid was the only person in the world who knew all about Elizabeth's crush on Todd. And that Elizabeth was hoping he would ask her to the Harvest Dance, the first event of the school year. The dance was always planned by the guys on the football team—a tradition that had started a few years back when the cheerleaders and boosters had complained that guys never helped out with dances. But after Todd's phone call this morning, Elizabeth was starting to wonder if she even had a shot. Part of her wanted to tell Enid what had happened, but a bigger part did not want to go there again. Not yet, anyway. Maybe it would turn out to be nothing.

Enid smiled. "Don't worry. He will."

"Maybe. We'll see," Liz said. "But forget about me. We're talking about you. What else did you and Ronnie talk about?"

Enid was just about to reply when her eyes opened wide with fear. "Look out!" She grabbed Elizabeth and yanked her backward onto the grass. All Elizabeth saw was a blur of red zipping past them. Then there was a screech of tires. When she sat up again, she saw that a red Jeep Wrangler had just parked in the empty spot next to Bruce's convertible.

Jessica!

Elizabeth glanced at the spot where she'd parked the car two minutes ago. Empty. She quickly checked her jacket pocket for her keys. Gone. She felt as if she'd just been smacked across the back of her head. No wonder Jessica had had such a sudden change of heart! She'd only hugged Elizabeth to lift the keys.

"Excuse me. I have a sister to kill," Elizabeth said, getting up and brushing herself off.

"Okay! But Liz, don't tell anybody about—"

"Don't worry. I won't!"

Elizabeth headed for her sister, who was now flirting shamelessly with Bruce Patman, leaning back against the rear bumper of his car. This time she was really going to unload on Jessica. Where did the girl get off, manipulating her like that? It was just so infuriating. So, so, *so*—

"Hey! What's the rush?"

Elizabeth stopped in her tracks. She'd been so focused on her sister, she hadn't noticed someone jogging to catch up with her. A tall, ridiculously perfect-looking someone.

"Oh, hey . . . hi, Todd," Elizabeth said. Suddenly, she was sweating.

He paused in front of her, gripping the strap on his backpack, and smiled. Elizabeth's knees actually felt weak as she looked into his warm brown eyes. She wished she had something to lean on. Something other than his gorgeous, athletic, tan bod. Of course, that would've been nice too. . . .

"Hey. I'm glad I caught you," he said. "I wanted to talk to you before class."

Elizabeth heard Jessica's lilting laugh and was temporarily overcome with anger again. "Why?"

Todd's face creased with confusion. Elizabeth wanted to smack herself. Was she really standing here in the middle of the school parking lot being rude to Todd Wilkins?

"Wow. You really are always in reporter mode. Straight to the point," Todd joked.

Relieved, Elizabeth laughed. "Sorry. I've just had a weird morning. What's up?"

"It's cool. I was just wondering if—"

At that moment, the bell rang. Everyone around them started hustling toward the front door.

"Perfect timing," Todd said.

"It's okay. What did you want to ask me?" Elizabeth said hopefully.

Todd looked around, suddenly seeming nervous. "We're gonna be late. Can we talk later, maybe? Will you be around after football practice?"

"Sure. I have some work to do at the Oracle anyway," Elizabeth replied. The school's news Web site took up a lot of Elizabeth's time, but she loved writing both her news stories and her anonymous blog, the Insider.

Today she'd be even happier than usual to stay late if it meant she would get to see Todd afterward. "How about I meet you under the clock at five?"

"It's a plan," Todd said, smiling as he backed toward the school. "See you then, Liz."

"See you then," she repeated.

He turned and jogged off, and Elizabeth couldn't tear her eyes away. He was even beautiful while running. When her heartbeat finally returned to normal, she suddenly remembered Jessica. She whirled around but found that the Roadster and the Jeep were deserted. Jessica had already slipped away.

● ● ●

"*Gastar.* To spend," Elizabeth muttered, looking down at her Spanish notebook as she walked to class. She had a vocab and conjugation quiz in about two minutes and needed some last-second cramming. "*Gritar.* To shout."

She was just turning a corner when Ken Matthews, captain of the football team, came barreling toward her at top speed, his head turned away from her.

"Watch—"

Ken slammed into her and her books went flying. He

did, however, catch the football one of his teammates had hurled at him.

"Out," Liz said morosely, staring down at the mess at her feet.

"Oops. Sorry, Liz!" Ken said jovially, flipping his blond hair out of his eyes. He didn't stop, however, and Elizabeth was left to pick up her things on her own. She crouched to the floor and tried not to grumble as everyone in the hallway stepped over and around her, no one bothering to help.

Why does Jessica never get caught in these embarrassing situations? she thought. *Oh, right. Because she's* Jessica. *And Ken Matthews would have stopped to help Jessica. If she dropped her books, there would be ten guys lined up to help her out.*

"Liz?"

Elizabeth looked up into the quizzical blue-green eyes of her twin. "Jess?" she said, mimicking her wondrous tone.

"What are you doing on the floor? Someone might think it's me grubbing around like that," Jessica said.

Don't kill her, Elizabeth thought. *Murder is still illegal in California.*

"So I guess that means you're not gonna help me,

then." Elizabeth grabbed her Spanish text as it tried to slip from her hands.

"It looks like you've got it under control. But I guess I'll have to tell you my news later," Jessica said.

"What news?"

"Just the best news ever," Jessica said with a grin.

Elizabeth suddenly felt nauseated. "Is it about the dance?"

"You'll see!" Jessica said, starting down the hall.

Gathering her stuff as quickly as possible, Elizabeth stood. "No! Tell me now." If this was bad news—Todd-related news—she just wanted to get it over with.

Jessica grinned and scurried on her toes back to Elizabeth, like a psyched-up ballerina. She grabbed Elizabeth's arm, nearly making her spill her books all over again, and leaned in.

"I think Todd Wilkins is going to ask me to the dance," she whispered.

Instantly, Elizabeth felt tears prick the corners of her eyes. "Why? Did he say something?"

"Not yet. But, I mean, first he calls this morning, and then he totally talked to me for the whole walk between English and chem," Jessica said. "He's never done *that* before."

"Oh. Well. That's . . ."

Horrible. Crushing. Completely and totally devastating.

"Great! I know! He is *so* hot, Liz. Can you just imagine how good we'd look together?" Jessica gushed.

Elizabeth could imagine it. Because they would look exactly as good together as *she* and Todd would look together, and Elizabeth had imagined that about a thousand times.

"Well. Gotta go! I'll see you later!" Jessica trilled.

"Later," Elizabeth muttered under her breath, since Jessica had already fluttered her fingers and run off. Suddenly, she felt as if she weighed ten thousand pounds, and was really wishing for her bed and her pillow and a nice, thick comforter to pull over her head. Unfortunately, there were still a few hours left before she'd get to go home and wallow.

Home. Right. Elizabeth paused and cursed herself under her breath. In all the gut-clenching disappointment, she'd forgotten to ask Jessica for the car keys.

• • •

Elizabeth still had one small hope to hold on to for the rest of the day: Todd was meeting her under the clock at five. He had wanted to talk to her about something so important that they'd made a date to meet up. Was it possible that Jessica could be wrong about Todd's feelings? Was it at all possible that he was waiting under the clock to ask Elizabeth to the dance?

Sitting in the Oracle office as Mr. Collins, the Web site advisor, slowly went over her latest article, Elizabeth checked her watch. It was already ten after five.

"Have somewhere you need to be?" Mr. Collins asked, raising his eyebrows in front of the computer screen.

"No! No. I'm . . . fine," Elizabeth said.

"Really? Because that's the tenth time you've checked your watch in two minutes," he said with a twinkle in his blue eyes. His sandy blond hair fell across his forehead and he flipped it back again. Mr. Collins looked way too young and hot to be a high school teacher. But while Jessica and her friends were constantly gabbing about how crush-worthy he was, Elizabeth respected him for his dedication—and she pretty much lived to impress him. Which was why she was so embarrassed to be caught all distracted.

"Is it?" Elizabeth squeaked.

"Go. This looks great. I'll post it on the site before I leave."

"Really?" Liz said, grabbing her books. "Because I can do it if—"

"Just go." Mr. Collins waved her off with a laugh.

"Thanks, Mr. C," Elizabeth said.

For the first time in her life, Elizabeth Wakefield broke the rules and ran in the school hallway.

Please still be there, she thought. *Please still be there and please ask me to the dance.*

If Jessica was wrong about this one little thing, Elizabeth would forgive her for everything—even for faking nice and swiping the car keys.

Elizabeth raced down the last flight of stairs and tore through the lobby. Outside, she headed straight for the tall, old-fashioned clock that stood in the circle at the center of the front drive. There were a few people milling around, including Cara Walker and some of Jessica's other cheerleading teammates, but she didn't see Todd. She scanned the parking lot, hoping to catch him if he was on his way to his car, and finally spotted him.

Her heart leapt, but then just as quickly nose-dived. Todd was getting into her very own Jeep Wrangler, laughing and chatting happily, with Jessica.

CHAPTER
3

"ANYBODY HOME?"

Elizabeth went to the top of the stairs to find her brother standing at the bottom, his battered duffel bag slung over his shoulder. Steven had gotten a little scruffier since moving out of the house and onto the Sweet Valley University campus at the beginning of September. But with his brown eyes and athletic build, he was still handsome, like a younger version of their father.

"You again?" Elizabeth joked.

"You must be that ugly Wakefield twin I hear so much

about," Steven replied with a smirk. "What's up? No hello?"

Elizabeth jogged down the stairs. "Only if I can get a hug, too."

Steven obliged, then looked at her quizzically. "What's the matter?"

"Oh, nothing," Elizabeth lied hastily. "It's just good to see you."

Steven dropped his duffel bag on the floor and slipped out of his leather jacket. "See me? I've been home every weekend for the past month."

"Yeah. What's that about, anyway?" Elizabeth asked. "Are you homesick? Big, bad Steven Wakefield can't make it out on the mean streets of SVU without his mommy?"

"Okay, that's enough out of you," Steven said, grabbing her in a headlock. "Come on. Let's see what you got to eat around here."

He dragged a laughing Elizabeth toward the kitchen at the back of the house, where he finally let her go. Feeling infinitely better, Liz headed for the fridge while Steven attacked the pantry.

"I've got chips!" Steven announced.

"I have salsa!" Elizabeth replied. "Oh! And shredded cheddar."

"Sweet! Bring it on!" Steven kicked the pantry door closed and popped open the bag of chips as they met at the table. "So, how are things on the home front these days?" Steven asked, dunking a chip into the salsa jar before Elizabeth even had a chance to set it down.

"Things are okay," Elizabeth replied. She dug some salsa out with a chip and sprinkled some cheese onto it. "The usual, I guess. School. The Web site. Homework. You know. Stuff."

"Stuff? What kind of stuff?" he asked, digging out another huge mound of salsa.

She crunched into her chip and sat back. Should she tell Steven about Todd? Or about Jessica? She sighed, hating to link those two names even in her mind. But she didn't want to be a whiner, and she definitely didn't want to put Steven in the middle.

"Nothing I can't handle. Don't worry your pretty little head about it," Elizabeth joked.

Steven took a deep breath and shook his head. "I am pretty, aren't I? It's a curse."

"Yeah. I bet you have a crowd of stalkers at SVU," Elizabeth said with a hint of sarcasm.

"That's why I have to come home every weekend," Steven joked back. "It's embarrassing. For them, I mean.

All the hair pulling and eye gouging. I want these girls to maintain some shred of self-respect."

"Okay. You have issues." Elizabeth pulled the salsa jar closer for another bite. "But seriously, why are you home for the fourth weekend in a row? Is everything okay at school?"

"Yeah. It's fine. I just like to see the family once in a while," Steven said, averting his eyes.

"Sure you do, Steve. And we're really grateful for the fifteen minutes you actually spend with us every weekend," Liz replied. "What I'm dying to know is where you're spending the other forty-seven and three-quarter hours."

"Impressive math skills, Liz. You should take that act on the road."

"Impressive subject-change attempt. But it didn't work."

Steven shrugged. "I hang out with the guys, you know? That kind of thing." Then he laughed. "When did you get so nosy?"

"I'm a reporter, remember? Nosy by nature," Elizabeth replied.

"Okay, moving on. . . . How're Mom and Dad?" Steven asked. "I've barely spoken to them this week."

"I know! They've been so busy I hardly see them. Mom's always rushing off to meet a client, and Dad has been spending all his time at the office with Marianna West," Elizabeth said.

"Marianna West?"

"Yeah. She's this new lawyer in his firm."

"Is she hot?" Steven asked, raising an eyebrow.

"Steven!"

"What? I'm just asking. If Dad's spending so much time with her . . ."

"Omigod. You're as bad as Jessica," Elizabeth said. *"If I were married, there's no way I'd let my husband spend so much time with a hot lawyer woman,"* she said, mimicking Jessica's voice.

Steven nearly choked on a chip. "Wow. That was dead on."

"I have lived every second of my life with the girl," Elizabeth pointed out. "Except for those first four minutes out of the womb." She heaved a dramatic sigh. "That was a peaceful time."

Steven cracked up laughing. "Well, if I know Jessica, her poor husband's gonna be on a leash."

At that moment the back door flew open and Jessica whirled in, smiling as only she could when her day had been absolute perfection.

"Steven!" she squealed, dropping her books on the counter and rushing to hug her brother. "I didn't know you were coming home."

Just the sight of her sister after everything Jessica had done that day made Elizabeth's blood boil. She got up from the table and went over to the sink to scrub something. Getting out her aggression by cleaning usually did the trick. Plus the running water had the added benefit of drowning out Jessica and Steven. Part of her was dying to know where Jessica and Todd had driven off to after school, but a bigger part wanted to spare herself the gory details. If Todd wanted Jessica, that was just fine. She would not stand in the way. Instead, she'd do the decent thing. Die.

"So, what're you doing this weekend?" Jessica asked her brother as Elizabeth clanked some pots and pans around in the sink. "Because I was thinking I could set you up with Cara Walker. She would be totally perfect for you."

Steven glanced at his watch. "Actually, I have plans. And I'm kind of already late for them," he said, getting up quickly.

"What, you have plans *all* weekend?" Jessica asked.

"Kind of," Steven hedged.

"Come on, Steven. What's wrong with Cara? She's

smart, she's the best tennis player in school, and she's totally hot. All the guys want her," Jessica said. "But she only wants you. That's a plus, right?"

Even her big brother wasn't immune to the usual tricks. Play to the ego. Worked every time.

"Sure, that's a plus," Steven replied. "I just think she's a little young for me." He looked at his watch again. "I'd better go."

Jessica narrowed her eyes at her brother. He was being way too evasive. And he was blushing. Was it possible that . . . ?

"All right. Who is she?" Jessica demanded.

Steven froze. "Who's who?"

"Who's the girl? You come home every weekend, but you're never here. You don't even bring laundry. You must be coming here to see someone," Jessica theorized. "So who is it? Someone from SVU that lives here? Hmmm . . . who do I know that goes to Sweet Valley University?"

"Jess, you're crazy. There's no one," Steven said. "But right now, I've really gotta go."

"Fine!" Jessica shouted after him as he hurried upstairs. "But I'm gonna figure it out! I have a talent for this kind of thing!" She turned to her sister, who was just turning off the water. "What's with him? Do you know who he's going out with?"

Elizabeth silently grabbed a towel and wiped her hands.

"Hello? I'm talking to you here!" Jessica said.

Elizabeth shot her a look of death and threw the towel on the counter.

"What the heck did I do now?" Jessica asked.

"Oh, I don't know. It's kind of hard for me to remember with all the blisters throbbing on my feet," Elizabeth said tartly.

"Okay. That makes no sense," Jessica replied.

"Jess! Thanks to you I had to walk all the way home from school in those stupid new sandals, which, by the way, I'm totally throwing out now. They're so uncomfortable."

"Oooh. Can I have them?" Jessica asked.

"Omigod. Can you *focus*?" Elizabeth shouted. "First you swipe the keys when you're grounded from driving. And then you ditch me! What's the matter with you?"

Oops! Jessica thought. *Well, there has to be a good way out of this one.* "Please, Liz! You ditched me!" she blurted out, going with the classic redirect. "I saw you get into a car with Enid and those guys after school and take off! You really should have told me you had plans, you know. I had to drive the car, and if Mom had seen me I could have gotten grounded for even longer."

"Jessica," Elizabeth said, her voice full of warning, "I didn't go anywhere after school. I was working in the Oracle office until after five, and then I saw *you* take off with Todd."

"Oh. I guess it was just someone else, then," Jessica said. "In that case, I forgive you. Now let's talk about Steven. He definitely has a girlfriend. Who do you think it is?" Jessica yanked open the refrigerator and grabbed a bag of grapes. "Do you think it's someone older?" she asked mischievously, turning and popping a grape into her mouth.

"I don't know, Jess. I don't want to talk about Steven right now. I want to talk about what happened after school," Elizabeth said. "Did you and Todd . . . go somewhere?"

Jessica rolled her eyes and dropped onto one of the stools at the center island. "Of course we went somewhere, Liz. We were in a car."

Elizabeth pulled her discarded towel to her and ran it through her fingers. "Where'd you go?"

"He had to pick up some decorations for the dance, so

I offered him a ride into town. He's so sweet, Liz. He opened doors for me all afternoon. Who does that?"

Elizabeth looked down at the counter. "Did he say anything about meeting someone . . . or waiting for someone after school?"

Jessica sat up straight and scratched an itch on her back. "No. I don't think so," she said casually. Todd had, in fact, said something about waiting for Liz, but Jessica had told him that Elizabeth had already left. "Now can we talk about Steve?"

"What about him?" Elizabeth said blankly.

"Liz! Our brother is having a secret love affair and you don't even care!" Jessica exclaimed.

"I care," Elizabeth protested. "But come on, Steven? If he had a girlfriend, he would tell us. In fact, he wouldn't be able to shut up about it."

"True, but still. He comes home but doesn't stay here. He never really says where he's going. It all adds up," Jessica said. "He's dating someone and he doesn't want us to know who it is, which, considering how very open-minded we are, means she must be pretty bad. I'm so going to figure this out."

"Count me out, Nancy Drew," Elizabeth said. "He's our brother. We should respect his privacy."

Jessica's face burned. Sometimes Elizabeth's high-and-mighty attitude was beyond irritating. "Whatever, Liz. I just want to help the guy. If he's going out with some loser, I'm going to tell him. Some of us can't be so cold and selfish when it comes to the happiness of the people we love."

She gave her stunned sister an angelic smile and grabbed her books before flouncing out of the room.

"Love *this*!" Elizabeth spat, throwing the balled-up towel across the kitchen, where it narrowly missed hitting her mother as she stepped through the back door.

Great. I have one small temper tantrum in, like, five years and my mom is here to witness it, she thought.

"Elizabeth? What's going on?" Alice Wakefield asked as she closed the door behind her.

"I thought you were coming home late," Elizabeth snapped.

Her mother paused, looking at Elizabeth as if she'd just morphed into a devil woman. "Nice attitude. I had some free time before my next meeting, so I went shopping. You could help me, you know."

"Sorry, Mom." Elizabeth took one of the brown bags from her mother's arms and put it on the table. "Nothing's going on. I was just cleaning and I thought I . . . uh . . . saw a spider on the towel," she improvised.

Mrs. Wakefield eyed the towel dubiously and placed the other grocery bag on the counter. "Uh-huh. What's really going on?"

Suddenly, Elizabeth wished she were five years old again. Then she could cry and pour out everything to her mother, who would make it all right. But that was then; this was now.

"Nothing, Mom. I told you." Elizabeth stormed past her mother and grabbed the towel again. Her heart pounded with frustration and anger. All she wanted to do was be alone so she could calm down.

"Sometimes it helps to talk about it," her mother said.

"There's nothing to talk about," Elizabeth groused.

"Right. That's why you're acting completely out of character."

Something inside Elizabeth snapped and she felt tears welling up in her eyes. "What? I have one little moment of anger and I've lost it? Because no. I'm not supposed to have feelings. I'm supposed to be Elizabeth Wakefield. Level-headed, responsible, sweet little Liz. Well, you know what that adds up to, Mom? Boring! I am the most boring person I know."

"Honey, calm down," Mrs. Wakefield said, reaching for her daughter's hand. But Elizabeth pulled back.

"Well, news flash, Mom. Even Elizabeth Wakefield gets angry sometimes, okay?" Liz rambled. "Especially when–"

"Whoa," Steven said as he came through the door. "What did I just walk in on?"

"Nothing," Elizabeth said, walking over to the sink. She grasped the edge of the counter and took a deep breath. She couldn't believe what she'd been about to do. She'd been on the verge of telling her mother everything. Every humiliating detail about her crush on Todd and how he apparently liked Jessica instead.

Get a grip, Liz. Don't be such a baby.

"Steven! I saw your car in the driveway. I didn't know you were coming home," Mrs. Wakefield said.

"I'm here and I'm gone, Mom," Steven said, giving her a quick kiss.

"Where are you going?" she asked.

"Out."

"Out? Where? With whom?" she asked.

"Just out, okay? Has privacy become a dirty word around here?" Steven asked. "The DA upstairs just grilled me for five minutes until her phone finally rang and she got distracted. Remind me to thank this Todd kid for calling if I ever meet him. He totally saved me."

Elizabeth's heart dropped. Todd had called Jessica

44

again? They were on the phone together right now? The tears escaped from her eyes before she could stop them. This was so unfair. Jessica got everything she wanted, and now she was getting everything *Liz* wanted too.

"Hey, Liz. Are you okay?" Steven asked.

"I'm fine," she replied. Then she ducked her head and ran past her brother and up the stairs before he or her mother could ask her anything else.

CHAPTER 4

ELIZABETH SAT IN the Oracle office at lunch, the cursor on the computer screen in front of her mocking her with its blinking. The Insider blog page sat open and completely empty in front of her. No matter how hard she tried, she could not make herself concentrate on the gossip column right now. Gossip wasn't her expertise anyway, but now there were too many more important things fighting for attention in her mind. Who was breaking up with whom and who'd been caught kissing behind the gym just could not compete.

Was Jessica right about Steven? Was he seeing some random girl behind their backs? And if so, why did he feel the need to keep it a secret from his entire family? And then there was her father and Marianna West. They had driven by her earlier that day, and Liz had lifted her hand to wave, but they had been so wrapped up in each other they hadn't even noticed her. And finally, of course, there was Todd.

With a sigh, Elizabeth slowly typed his name into the blog. For no reason. Just to stare at it. If only the bell hadn't rung the other day when he'd caught up to her in the parking lot. If they had had time to talk that morning, what would he have asked her? Would she and Todd be going out right now? Sitting in the cafeteria together? Holding hands in the hallway? Maybe even sharing a kiss behind the—

"Liz! Liz! I have an idea for, like, a headline!" Cara Walker announced, barreling into the room like a crazed bull.

Heart in her throat, Elizabeth quickly closed the blog window on her computer. No one was supposed to know who wrote the Insider. It was a Sweet Valley High tradition that if and when the mystery gossip blogger was unveiled, he or she was thrown fully clothed into the SVH pool. It happened every year, but Elizabeth was hoping to put off her own unveiling for as long as possible. Cara, however, seemed too excited to notice Liz's guilty behavior. She tossed her dark hair over her shoulder and hugged her books, her eyes bright.

"What is it?" Elizabeth asked her.

"Well, do you know who writes the Insider?" Cara asked.

Elizabeth swallowed hard and scoffed. "No one knows that, Cara. Except Mr. Collins."

"Okay, then tell Mr. Collins, I guess, and he can tell whoever it is," Cara said, waving a hand. "You ready?"

Elizabeth opened up a new Word document and poised her fingers over the keyboard. "Ready."

"Two of the hottest people in school have finally coupled up," Cara said. "The captain of the cheerleading squad has snagged the captain of the basketball team."

Elizabeth's fingers curled as her stomach clenched painfully. The words in front of her blurred. "What?"

"They're both captains! Isn't that just so cheesy it's cool?" Cara gushed. "I just think it could make a cute headline or whatever. I'm not big with words, but I bet the Insider could come up with something cute to do with it."

"Wait a minute, wait a minute," Elizabeth said, finally catching her breath. "You're talking about Jessica and Todd? They're a couple now? Since when?"

Cara rolled her eyes impatiently. "Everybody's talking about it. They're practically inseparable."

"Oh. Everybody's talking about it?" Liz said flatly.

"Well, yeah. It can't be news to you, right? You live with the girl," Cara said.

No. It's not news to me, Elizabeth thought.

"I'll make sure the Insider gets right on it," she said.

"Okay. Cool. See ya, Liz!" Cara trilled.

The second the door closed behind Cara, Liz's head hit her folded arms on the desk. She took a few deep breaths and tried to calm her aching heart.

"Okay, this is reality," she said aloud. "Just deal with it. Todd likes Jessica. *Todd* likes *Jessica*. Everybody knows it. Everybody's talking about it." She lifted her head and stared at the computer screen. "And it makes perfect sense. He's a hot jock. She's a hot jock. Why shouldn't they get together and make a hot jock couple?"

But he smiled at me *in the cafeteria. And he wanted to talk to* me *before school. Unless . . .*

Elizabeth thought back to the day Todd had smiled that smile that felt like it was just for her. She'd worn her hair down that day, hadn't she? And was that the day she'd borrowed that black graphic T-shirt from Jessica? She was almost sure of it. Oh God, was it possible . . . Had Todd thought he was smiling at Jessica?

Elizabeth closed her eyes and groaned. What was wrong with her? She'd been basing all her hopes on a case of mistaken identity. And the day he'd wanted to talk to her before school was the day he'd asked Jessica for help with dance decorations. Maybe that was why he'd wanted to talk to *her* in the first place. Of course. Ask responsible, dependable Liz for help organizing the dance. When she hadn't shown up and Jessica had offered to help in her place, he must have been so excited. He'd gotten to spend the afternoon with the girl he liked instead of that girl's dull sister.

Elizabeth shook her head, blinking back humiliated tears. It was time to face facts. Jessica liked Todd and Todd liked Jessica. Now all she had to do was blog about it.

Clearing her throat, Elizabeth opened the Insider window again, sat up straight, and started to type.

> Wondering who'll be the hottest couple at the upcoming Harvest Dance? How about a certain model-material wide receiver/basketball captain and the beautiful blond captain of the cheerleading squad? That

```
coupling should be hot enough
to melt right through the dance
floor.
```

Liz sat back and stared at the words.

They're perfect for each other, she told herself. *I'm happy for them. I really am.*

She swallowed the sob that was trying to make its way up her throat. Suddenly, the door was flung open again and Liz minimized the screen.

"Mr. Collins!" John Pfeiffer called out, racing through the door. John, the sports editor of the Oracle, paused when he saw Elizabeth sitting there, looking miserable.

"Hey, John," she said, her voice cracking slightly. She cleared her throat again. "Everything okay?"

"Oh, hey, Liz. Yeah. It's just, I'm a total idiot. We're doing the football team profiles, and I somehow deleted the only picture we have of Todd Wilkins," he said. "Do you have any idea what class he has next period? I might have to track him down and try to do something with my camera phone."

Modern Civ, Elizabeth thought automatically. *He has Modern Civ next period.*

Then she wanted to throttle herself for being so pathetic.

"No, I don't know what he has next period," she said, getting up and grabbing her books. "Why would I know that?"

"Okay, chill. I'll just find out at the office," John said, looking slightly disturbed.

"Good. Do that. I have to go now," Elizabeth said as she turned off her computer.

Then, embarrassed beyond belief, she ducked out of the room and walked right into Todd Wilkins himself. And he was walking with Jessica. Elizabeth's heart crumbled. How cruel could the universe actually be?

"Hey, Liz!" Todd said brightly.

"John's in there looking for you," she told him.

Then, without a second glance at her sister, she turned around and speed-walked away, headed for the nearest bathroom and the privacy of a nice, locked stall.

"My sister," Jessica said, throwing up a hand. "Always rushing off to meet some guy or other."

"Really?" Todd said. "Liz?"

"Are you kidding? She's, like, ridiculously popular," Jessica said. "Not like me. I mean, I am just ridiculously *un*popular. Especially lately. I mean, it seems like everybody has a date for the dance except for me. Everyone but me."

Todd stared down the hall after Elizabeth as if Jessica

hadn't said a word. Which made her nerves sizzle. Jessica was not used to being ignored.

"I was coming up here to apologize about ditching her last week," he said.

"Todd, come on. It's no big deal," Jessica said. "Besides, I already told her. You had to go before the store closed that night," she fibbed. "It wasn't your fault she was late to meet you."

"Yeah, I guess. I just feel bad," Todd told her.

"Well, don't worry about it. Believe me, if I know Liz she's already forgotten all about it. She has about ten million other things going on," Jessica said. "Not to mention ten million other guys to meet up with."

Todd laughed. "Yeah, right." Then, when Jessica didn't laugh as well, his brow creased. "You are kidding, right?"

"Not when it comes to Liz," Jessica said. "I, on the other hand, don't even have one. Not even one single guy to, say, go to the dance with."

"The dance?" Todd asked distractedly.

"Yeah. You know, the Harvest Dance?" Jessica said, psyched to finally be off the topic of Liz. "You're going, right? Well, obviously you're going. You're organizing the thing."

"Yeah. Of course," Todd said. "So you think Liz already has a date, then?"

Jessica felt her skin start to grow hot, but she took a deep breath and held back her ire. She could not blow up at Todd Wilkins. She had a feeling that showing her temper would scare him off for good, possibly right into the arms of her more levelheaded twin.

"I'm telling you, Todd. I just cannot keep up with all her men," Jessica said. "But if you don't have a date, and I don't have a date . . ."

Come on, already! I'm spoon-feeding you here! she thought.

Todd really looked at Jessica for the first time, and his brown eyes finally, *finally* seemed to register her message.

"Oh, right. If you don't have a date and I don't have a date—"

That's right. Get there. Get there. . . .

"Hey, Todd!" John Pfeiffer said, emerging from the Oracle office. "Thank God, dude. You got a second to take a picture for the Web site?"

"Oh, uh, sure," Todd said. "Sorry, Jess. I gotta go," he said, stepping around her. "But don't worry about the dance. There's tons of time to find someone."

Then he turned and walked off down the hall with John, leaving Jessica stunned behind him.

"You have *got* to be kidding me," she said aloud.

What the heck was going on around here? Any other guy would have been drooling at her feet by now. But Todd . . . it was like he didn't even know she existed.

Which, much to her irritation, only made her want him more.

CHAPTER

5

"UNBELIEVABLE. I NEVER thought I'd see the day."

"What?" Jessica shot an irritated look at the pimped-out electric blue VW Eos that had pulled up alongside her. It had running lights and racing stripes, just like something out of *The Fast and the Furious,* and the engine was making more noise than a garbage truck. But it wasn't the car that was intriguing so much as the driver. The infamous Rick Andover. Dark hair. Dark stubble. Piercing blue eyes. A Sweet Valley High dropout with a reputation for running through girls and red lights with equal lack of care. Trouble with a capital "T."

"I'm just saying, *the* Jessica Wakefield walking home from school alone?"

Jessica paused and slowly smiled. Now, this was more like it. Unlike Todd, who seemed to look right through her, Rick looked her up and down as if she were the only girl he'd ever seen.

"Have you taken it all in yet?" Jessica asked coyly.

Rick smirked. "Not even close."

Jessica's heart skipped a beat. Flirting with Rick was dangerous, she knew. And she liked it.

"Get in," he said, tilting his head toward the passenger seat. "Unless your mommy told you never to take rides with strangers."

Poor Rick. He had no idea who he was dealing with.

"Like that would ever stop me," Jessica said.

She strutted around the car and slipped into the low bucket seat. Her skirt rode up and she adjusted it slightly, then pressed her knees together and tilted them toward Rick. It had the desired effect. He couldn't tear his eyes off her.

"I thought you were driving me home," Jessica said giddily.

Rick finally managed to look at her face, and smiled. "I think I'm gonna like you."

"I know you are."

With a laugh, Rick took off, shooting ahead of an old Taurus and through a yellow light. Jessica's heart raced, and she tried not to clutch the seat. Soon, however, she got used to the thrill of speeding through town and relaxed. This was actually kind of fun. Like a roller coaster.

"I don't let just any strange girl in my car, you know," Rick said as he took a corner, tires squealing.

Jessica smirked. Everyone knew Rick had a different girl in his car every day of the week. The girls were all gorgeous. Most were older. She'd even seen a few of them herself. But today, she was the girl in the passenger seat everyone was gaping at. And it felt good.

"Why's that?" she asked, playing along.

"Well, how do I know you won't try to take advantage of my innocence?" he teased.

Jessica laughed. "Don't worry. I'm fighting off the urge to attack you."

He shot her a look that said he was just barely fighting the urge himself. "Don't fight too hard. I'm not used to taking no for an answer."

"Neither am I," Jessica replied smoothly.

At that moment, she was reminded of Todd's indifference, and a shot of irritation hit her hard. She wished he could see her now, tooling around in Rick's notorious ride. Maybe he would even be jealous.

Rick turned his car onto a side road, doing fifty in a thirty-five zone. "So I'll pick you up at eight," he said.

"What?"

"You. Me. Tomorrow night. We should celebrate this once-in-a-lifetime event, don't you think?"

"Tomorrow's a school night," Jessica said without thinking, then wanted to smack herself.

Rick laughed. "Mommy and Daddy won't let you come out to play, huh?"

God, how humiliating. Who did she think she was, Elizabeth? Jessica tried to think of a way to save the situation. Something, anything, cool to say. Then it hit her.

"Like that would ever stop me," she repeated, smiling flirtatiously.

"That's what I like to hear." He looked her up and down and her skin tingled. There was something about that self-assuredness, those knowing blue eyes, that made Jessica's mind go all fuzzy.

"So, eight, then?" she said.

"I'll be waiting," he replied.

"Where should I meet you?" Jessica asked.

"Right here," he answered, jerking his car to a noisy

stop just around the corner from her house. "This is where you live, right?"

Jessica stared at him. "How did you know that?"

"I know where all the hottest girls live," he replied. "It's like radar."

Jessica felt a blush in every inch of her body. Rick was good. Maybe he wasn't Todd Wilkins, but he could be fun.

"Okay, then. I'll see you tomorrow," she said, opening the door.

"Wait." Rick grabbed her hand, stopping her, and Jessica's heart swooped. She turned to look at him and he leaned toward her. "Don't I get anything for the ride?"

Before Jessica could even respond, he reached behind her neck with the other hand and pulled her to him for a quick but heart-stopping kiss. When Jessica stood back again, she could hardly focus. Her senses were filled with the scents of leather and gasoline and the taste of Rick's passionate kiss.

"Where are we going tomorrow?" she asked as she got out of the car. She felt as if she had to say something to keep from looking like an overwhelmed amateur.

"You'll see."

He gunned the engine and she slammed the door.

With a squeal of tires he swerved onto the road and around the corner, just missing a blue Explorer turning onto Calico Drive. Jessica's heart leapt into her throat. Rick had almost taken out her mother! She turned around quickly and walked toward her house, trying to make it look as if she'd been walking all along. Her mother pulled past her and into the driveway.

"Hey, Mom!" Jessica said.

"Hi. Did you see that?" her mother asked, clearly freaked. "That car almost killed me back there."

Jessica flushed. "Uh, no. Didn't see it."

Her mother shook her head and slammed her car door. "Drivers like that on the road . . . ," she said with unusual vehemence.

"Mom. Calm down. You're fine," Jessica said.

"I'm sorry, honey," Mrs. Wakefield said as they headed for the front door. "I'm just all wound up today, I guess. And that did not help."

Jessica followed her mother into the house. It wasn't just today. Her mother had been tense a lot lately. Was it because her husband had been hanging out with Hot Lawyer Lady so much? Did Mrs. Wakefield suspect something too?

A hard knot of dread formed in Jessica's stomach. If her mother suspected her dad was cheating, that just made it all the more real. Great. Two minutes ago she'd been all aflutter from the encounter with Rick Andover, and now that feeling was completely gone.

Thanks a lot, Dad, Jessica thought.

Sometimes she really hated reality.

● ● ●

"Hey, Jess, can I get those jeans back? I want to wear them tomorrow."

Elizabeth paused in the doorway of her sister's bedroom. Jessica stood in front of her full-length mirror in a black miniskirt and a low-cut halter top, a different shoe on each foot.

"Whoa. I thought you were going to the library to study," Elizabeth said.

She saw her jeans sticking out from under Jessica's bed and snatched them. Jessica selected a pot of lip gloss from her dresser and dabbed it on with her fingertip. She leaned back to examine herself in the mirror, then gave Elizabeth a sly smile.

"Liz, when was the last time I actually went to the library?" she asked.

Elizabeth considered. "I think there was story time and a cookie involved."

"Exactly. Can you keep a secret?"

"Always," Elizabeth replied, even though she had a sneaking suspicion this was not a secret she wanted to hear.

"I have a date," Jessica whispered, her aquamarine eyes sparkling with mischief. "Swear you will not tell Mom."

Liz swallowed hard. *Yep. Definitely did not want to hear this.* "With who?"

Jessica turned toward her reflection again, lifting one foot, then the other. "Which shoe do you like better. This one, or this one?"

"Jessica," Elizabeth hissed, her heart pounding frantically. "Who are you going out with dressed up like—"

With a knowing smile, Jessica slipped out of the lower-heeled shoe and pushed her foot into the high-heeled sandal. "A lady never kisses and tells."

A lady also doesn't go out looking like that *on a Tuesday night,* Elizabeth thought.

Jessica giggled with excitement and dove into her closet, coming out with a cardigan sweater to cover her sexy shirt until she got out of the house. Elizabeth watched her sister, feeling sick to her stomach. She was going out with Todd. She had to be. They were a couple now, right? Everyone was talking about it.

Still, it didn't make sense. If Jessica wanted to go out with a guy like Todd Wilkins—even on a Tuesday night—she wouldn't have to keep it a secret and she wouldn't have to sneak out.

But then again, that was just Jessica. Turning it into a big mystery and sneaking out of the house just made the whole thing more exciting for her. And Elizabeth could only imagine how exciting it would be for Todd when he saw her sister in that outfit.

"Well, have fun," Elizabeth said, her shoulders slumping as she left the room.

"Oh, don't worry about that, Liz," Jessica called after her. "I definitely will."

CHAPTER

6

RICK'S CAR WAS already idling at the curb as Jessica approached. She slipped out of her cardigan sweater and tossed it over her arm. Through the windshield, she could see Rick's piercing eyes taking her in. This was going to be an interesting night.

"You're late," he said as she opened the door and slid into the seat. Slowly, he looked her up and down. "But it was totally worth it."

"Wasn't it, though?" Jessica said.

With a grin, Rick leaned in and covered her mouth with his. Jessica kissed him back, surprised. He tasted of cigarettes and . . . something else. Mouthwash? It had to be mouthwash.

"Let's hit it," he said, pulling away.

Jessica's stomach dropped as he peeled away from the curb, heading for the winding coastal highway. This time she did grip the underside of her seat, but she made sure to turn her body so that Rick couldn't tell.

"So . . . where are we going?" she asked as he merged onto the highway without so much as a glance in the mirror. He looked at her almost mockingly. "Oh, right. I'll see," she said.

"You learn fast," he said. "Can't wait to see what else you're good at."

Jessica felt a shiver of excitement and then a twinge of trepidation. She had always thought that all those stories about Rick Andover and his conquests were embellished rumors, but what if they were actually true? Would she be able to hold him off? She took a deep breath and looked out the window, watching the fence posts whipping by.

Don't worry about it, she told herself. *You can handle any guy.* And if worse came to worst, she always had her cell phone.

Ten minutes later, Rick pulled his car off the main highway and careened past a whole slew of Do Not Enter and Road Closed signs. Instantly, Jessica's skin started to tingle. She knew where they were going now. This was Coast Road, the old coastal highway that had been closed down after an earthquake took out most of its bridges years ago. She had heard that a bunch of people from all over the area came here to drag race every week, but she'd never believed it. The whole thing had just seemed too ripped-from-the-movie-screen to be true.

"Are we going to race?" Jessica asked. Her heart pounded with a potent mix of fear and excitement. Her mother would kill her if she knew where Jessica was right now, but she didn't care. This could be the coolest thing ever.

"You catch on fast," Rick replied.

"People really do that?"

Rick laughed sarcastically. "How naïve are you?"

At that moment, the car rounded a bend and Jessica was nearly blinded by hundreds of headlights. Parked in the dirt along the road were dozens and dozens of tricked-out autos, each one more *Pimp My Ride* than the last. All kinds of people milled around smoking, drinking from dark bottles, and checking out each other's cars. Jessica sat up, peering at the fabulously sleek and crazy cars, feeling as if she were driving through a theme-park auto safari. Rick revved his engine and a few guys walked up to the car to slap his hand.

"Hey. Look what Andover brought," one burly, bearded guy said, poking his head through the window to check Jessica out. Jessica pressed back into her seat, away from his leer.

"No touching the merchandise," Rick said with a smile.

Which, while offensive, did the job. The guy laughed and walked off.

"Thanks," Jessica said.

Rick didn't reply. He drove to the end of the line and parked next to a purple race car with its engine on the outside. Rick got out of the car and greeted his group of friends. Taking a deep breath, Jessica quickly followed. By the time she got to Rick's side he was already swigging brown liquid out of a bottle.

"Everyone, this is Jessica Wakefield," Rick announced, slinging his arm over Jessica's shoulders. "Jessica, this is everyone."

"Hi," Jessica said, tossing her hair back and trying not to look intimidated.

"Wow. Really upping your style, huh, Andover?" one multiply pierced guy asked.

"I do what I can," Rick said.

Jessica was confused but made sure not to let on. She watched as Rick tipped the bottle toward his lips again. "So, who're we racing?" she asked.

"It's you and me against Donny here and his girl Blaine," Rick said, pointing at Mr. Piercing. Blaine stepped up, all vinyl clothes and big hair, and looked Jessica up and down with obvious mirth.

"Cool," Jessica said. She turned to face Rick and lowered her voice. "But, uh, if you want to win, you might want to lay off that," she said, glancing at the bottle.

Rick laughed loudly, as did all his friends who had overheard.

"Well, well. She's a pure one," Donny said. He came up behind Jessica and slipped his hands over her shoulders, giving them a quick knead with his cold, dirty fingers. Jessica instantly flinched.

"What's your problem?" she spat at him.

More laughter and a few "ooohs." Jessica was starting to feel as if there was something going on here. Something she was not aware of. And she hated being out of the know.

"And lively, too!" Donny said, nodding. "What do I have to do to get her in my car, Andover?"

"Sorry, man," Rick said as he pulled Jessica closer. "She's all mine."

"Rick. I need to talk to you," Jessica said as she wriggled out of his arms.

She yanked him away from the crowd, which was easy to do because he was now totally drunk. Something she should've picked up on much sooner.

"Whoa. Whoa. Chill, girl," Rick said, raising his hands.

"What are you thinking?" Jessica said through clenched teeth, her anger barely masking her terror. "You can't race tonight! Not like this."

Rick laughed, long and loud. "Well, look who's got her stop sign out now. I thought you were looking for a little adventure."

"This is not adventure," Jessica said. "This is insane. Driving this road is dangerous during the day, let alone at night when you're too drunk to stand."

"Don't worry, babe. I'm a pro. And I'm gonna win. Then you and me can have a little fun."

"That's it," Jessica snapped, yanking her cell phone out of her bag. "I'm outta here."

She stormed past him and started to dial Elizabeth's phone, but her hand was shaking so badly she couldn't even hit the speed-dial button. Rick caught up to her quickly, grabbed the phone from her hand, and turned it off. Jessica whirled on him and found all his friends looming behind him.

"You're not going anywhere," Rick said menacingly.

Jessica opened her mouth. To beg. To scream. To spit. To do something. But before she could, Rick grabbed her arm. Hard.

This was it. This was the last moment of her life as she knew it.

And then a siren split the air.

● ● ●

Mayhem ensued. Cars zipped off in every direction, kicking up dirt and dust and nearly running down spectators. Some people ran. Others jumped headfirst into moving vehicles. Jessica just stood there, stunned and unable to process anything, until a police officer jogged over to her.

"Miss? Are you all right?" he asked, looking into her eyes.

Jessica heard Rick shouting and cursing. She turned and found a cop dragging him out of his car by his arm and slamming him up against the side.

"Miss? Do your parents know you're here?" the police officer asked.

"No," Jessica said, shaking her head. "I didn't know . . . I didn't know where he was taking me."

"Where who was taking you?" the cop asked.

Jessica looked past him at Rick, and he turned to see who was there. "Rick Andover. You came here with him?"

"Yes, but I didn't—"

"It's okay. I believe you. This isn't the first time this has happened. Now let me get your name so I can call your parents."

Jessica felt her brain kick into action over her shock. "No! Please, please don't call them. They'll kill me."

"I doubt that. I'm sure they'll just be happy that you're safe," he said, his tone softening slightly. "Now, your name?"

Oh, God. I am so dead.

"Miss? I really must insist—"

Jessica swallowed hard. She covered her face with her hands. Someone nearby was cursing, and she heard the distinct sounds of retching. "It's . . . it's Wakefield," she said.

"Of course, Wakefield. I knew you looked familiar," the cop said. "Elizabeth, right? You're friends with my little sister Emily."

Jessica wrenched her eyes open. She stared at his name tag. It read MAYER.

"Emily Mayer?" she said. Emily was the drummer for Valley of Death, the one good band Sweet Valley High had produced in the last million years. She and Liz hung out on occasion.

"Yeah. You were at her sweet sixteen last year," the officer said.

"Actually, I–"

Actually, I wasn't invited, Jessica thought. Not that she'd cared at the time. It had been a smallish sleepover party–totally juvenile–and Emily wasn't exactly important in the social scheme of SVH.

"Okay, Elizabeth," the officer said. "Let's get you home."

The sound of the word "home" brought such an overwhelming sense of relief, Jessica didn't even think to correct him. She gratefully slid into the backseat of his cruiser and leaned her head back. That was when the tears finally started to flow. The thought of what had almost happened overcame her. She could have been killed. All because she had gotten into Rick Andover's car.

I'm sure they'll just be happy you're safe, Officer Mayer had said. Little did he know they already *thought* she was safe, in the library studying. They were going to completely freak if they found out the truth.

A little while later, the police cruiser pulled up in front of Jessica's house. She wiped her eyes as her heart hit her throat. This was it. The moment of truth. Officer Mayer got out of the car and came around to open her door. Jessica was frozen with fear. She could not walk up to her front door with a cop. Her life would be over. The door popped open and in rushed the cool night air.

"I can't," she said. "They'll kill me."

He sighed and crouched next to the door so she could see him. "Listen," he said, giving her a long, hard look. "I'm going to let you off this time with a warning. I believe you didn't intend to be out there with those people, and I believe in second chances."

"Really?" Jessica was so elated she practically jumped

out of the car. "Thank you *so* much, Officer! You won't regret this, I swear. It'll never happen again."

"It had better not," he said. "From now on, stay away from Rick Andover and that posse of his. I know what goes on out there. Racing that road is dangerous, and the way those kids drink means it's only a matter of time before we have a real tragedy. That's not a crowd to be messing around with. I hope you know that."

"I know," Jessica said, shuddering. She pulled her sweater tightly around herself, realizing what a close call she'd had. "Thanks."

"Now go on inside," he said with a brief smile as he got back in the car. "And remember, Elizabeth, I don't believe in *third* chances."

Jessica blinked when he called her Elizabeth. She'd almost forgotten the mix-up in all the life-passing-before-her-eyes trauma. "Oh, I'm not—"

But he had already slammed the door and pulled away.

Well, no harm, no foul. There won't even be a record of this, Jessica thought, turning toward her house.

She took a deep breath and sighed, suddenly exhausted. Thank God that was over. Blinded by her overwhelming relief, she didn't even see the girl on the other side of the street, standing there stunned with her dog straining against the leash, groping for her cell phone with her free hand.

This was exactly the kind of mind-blowing gossip Caroline Pearce just *loved* to share.

CHAPTER
7

ELIZABETH GLANCED OUT her bedroom window to check for Enid's car. All morning she'd kept a low profile, hiding from her sister so she wouldn't have to hear all the gory details of her date with Todd. She could hear Jessica banging around in her room, but luckily, for once, her twin hadn't barreled in demanding to borrow something or asking if she looked fat. In another minute Enid would be here and Liz would be free. She wouldn't even have to drive to school with Jessica, who would be left to beg for their mother's permission to take the Jeep.

With a sigh, Liz looked around her room, wishing she could just fake sick and stay here and not have to see

Todd at all. This room was her haven. She had chosen everything herself—the off-white carpeting, the soft cream color on the walls, the bed piled high with colorful silk and velvet pillows. Against one wall was the large table Elizabeth used as a desk, with her laptop in the center. The desk was flanked by bookcases, packed to the gills with everything from classic novels to modern bestsellers to plays and poetry collections. Liz liked to read everything she could get her hands on. If only she could just grab one of those books and curl up on her bed.

There was a honk outside the window and Elizabeth jumped. She grabbed her messenger bag and raced out of the room, nearly taking down her sister in the middle of the hallway.

"Liz!" Jessica exclaimed.

"Sorry! Enid's waiting for me," Elizabeth said.

"Wait! I was just coming to talk to you!" Jessica protested.

"No time. We want to get to school early to finish cramming for Russo's test," Elizabeth said.

"We have a test today?" Jessica asked.

"Yeah. You were at the library late last night studying for it, remember?" Liz said sarcastically.

Jessica's expression darkened. "Oh yeah. Right. Liz, about that. Just give me one second to—"

Elizabeth's heart constricted. At that moment Enid honked again. Perfect timing. Liz would have to thank her later. "Sorry. Gotta go. See you in school."

"Well, how am I supposed to get there? I'm not allowed to drive!" Jessica called after her.

"When has that ever stopped you?" Elizabeth replied.

She heard Jessica say something else, but it was too late. Elizabeth was already down the stairs and out the door. Saved from hearing her sister gush about Todd for at least the next eight hours.

● ● ●

"Do you think he's going to test us on cell structure again? You know how he lives for cell structure," Enid said as she and Elizabeth got out of the car in the school parking lot.

"He wants us to know it in our sleep, so my guess is yes," Elizabeth said.

She gazed down at her notebook as they crossed the lawn toward school, happy to be thinking about anything other than Todd and Jessica. Somebody whistled and she looked up automatically. A bunch of guys nearby were staring at her, grinning and checking her out.

"Didn't know you had it in you, Wakefield," Bruce Patman said, smirking.

"What?" Elizabeth asked, baffled.

"Come on, Liz," Enid said, pulling her away.

"Wait, what's he talking about?" Elizabeth said.

"Liz. It's Bruce Patman. Do you really want to know what he meant?" Enid asked.

Elizabeth smiled. "Good point."

Most of the girls at Sweet Valley High would have killed to talk to the gorgeous, rich star of the tennis team, but Liz and Enid were not most girls. Bruce was so shallow that on a sunny day Liz could see right through him.

"So, Liz. Is there anything you wanted to talk to me about?" Enid asked quietly as they walked toward one of the benches in front of the school.

"Like what?" Elizabeth asked.

"Like, I don't know . . . something," Enid said.

Elizabeth laughed and placed her bag on her lap as she sat. "Okay, you're going to have to dispense with the cryptic messages. What's up?"

"Nothing. It's just . . . if you don't want to talk about it, that's fine. I get it. But I just want you to know that I'm here for you. We're best friends. No matter what."

"Enid, you're freaking me out here. Am I dying or something?" Elizabeth joked.

"Everyone makes mistakes. Believe me. I know," Enid said seriously. "So I just want *you* to know that it doesn't matter to me. You don't have to worry about losing my friendship. Ever."

"Ooookay. Thanks," Elizabeth said, reaching up to feel Enid's forehead.

"What're you doing?" Enid asked.

"Just checking to see if you have a fever."

Suddenly, a shadow fell over them. Elizabeth looked up to find Enid's crush, Ronnie Edwards, hovering there with a sour expression on his face. This didn't look good.

"Hey, Enid. Can I talk to you?" he said.

"Uh, sure," Enid replied.

"Hi, Ronnie," Elizabeth said brightly, hoping to break whatever tension there was between him and her friend. Ronnie just cast her a sidelong glance that was not at all friendly.

"We're going to be late for homeroom," Ronnie told Enid.

"Okay. I'll see you later, Liz!" Enid jumped up and walked off with Ronnie, whispering to him as they went.

"Okay. See ya," Elizabeth said. Then she sat back, completely baffled. First Bruce made that weird remark, then Enid started babbling about undying friendship, and then Ronnie ignored her? What was up with everybody today?

• • •

"Why were you talking to her?" Ronnie asked through his teeth.

Enid's heart lurched. "What do you mean?"

"Everybody's talking about her, Enid," Ronnie said. "Do you really want to be associated with her? Drinking and driving is—"

"Ronnie! You haven't even heard her side of the story yet," Enid protested.

"Please. Caroline saw the whole thing with her own eyes. She heard the cop warn her about messing around with Rick Andover and his friends," Ronnie said. "If you keep hanging out with her, people are going to start thinking you're into that crap too."

"Liz is not into that crap," Enid said firmly. "It's all a rumor. Do you believe everything you hear?"

Please say no. Please say you're not going to judge her based on this.

"When a friend of mine tells me she saw it herself, then yeah. I do," Ronnie said.

"Well, Liz is *my* friend, and until she tells me otherwise, I'm giving her the benefit of the doubt."

"Fine," Ronnie said, narrowing his eyes. The bell rang and he turned away from her. "See you later, Enid."

He didn't even pause when she called after him.

● ● ●

"Steven, you were supposed to be back at school two days ago!" Alice Wakefield yelled from the kitchen. "What is going on with you?"

"Chill out, Mom! I told you. I didn't miss anything important," Steven replied.

Elizabeth paused at the front door. Her mother and brother were fighting? Just one more freakish occurrence on the most freakish day of her life. All day long, conversations had stopped when she entered rooms and kids had been shooting her strange looks in the hallway. Then Mr. Collins had been all mysterious about this issue with the school's football field and a hearing at the school board meeting tonight. It was like she'd gone to bed in a normal world and woken up on an alternate planet.

"That's not the point. You keep going out at all hours. You won't tell anyone what you're doing. Your father and I are very concerned about you."

"I didn't know you and Dad had time for anything other than work these days," Steven shot back.

In the foyer, Elizabeth winced. That was a low blow.

"Steven!"

"Sorry, Mom. I'm just sick of the third degree," Steven replied tersely. "I've gotta go. I'll see you Friday."

Elizabeth finally entered the kitchen just as Steven was going out the back door.

"Bye, Steve," she said.

"Later, Liz. Bye, Mom," he said, and was gone.

"What's up with him?" Elizabeth asked.

"I was hoping you could tell me," her mother said with a sigh.

At that moment, Elizabeth's cell phone rang. She pulled it from her bag and checked the caller ID. It was Enid. Elizabeth's pulse raced. She'd been wanting to get her friend alone all day to ask her what that bizzare conversation had been about this morning.

"I have to take this, Mom. Sorry," she said.

"There's a casserole in the freezer for you and Jessica!" Mrs. Wakefield called as Liz headed for the stairs. "Your father and I both have dinner meetings, so we'll be home late."

"Okay!" Liz called back. She jogged upstairs as she answered the phone. "Enid?"

"Hey, Liz." Her friend sounded morose.

"Okay, you have got to tell me what the heck is going on," Elizabeth said, closing her bedroom door behind her. "I was the human conversation killer today."

"Are you sitting down?" Enid asked.

Liz perched on the vintage settee she'd rescued from a secondhand shop last year. "I am now."

"Well, there are some kind of sick rumors going around. . . ."

Elizabeth clutched a pillow in her hand as Enid told her the story. By the time her friend was done, she could barely breathe.

"I don't believe this. Street racing? Drinking and driving? Enid! I've never even talked to Rick Andover in my life!"

"Caroline said she saw you, Liz," Enid said tentatively. "She said the cops dropped you off and the policeman called you by name. She said you're on probation or something. Something about three strikes . . . ?"

Elizabeth got up and walked to her window. This was a nightmare. A complete and total nightmare.

"Oh my God, Enid," she said suddenly, her breath catching in her throat. "What about Todd? Do you think he heard about this?"

There was a long pause. "Liz, I hate to say it, but I think everyone heard about this."

Tears welled up in Elizabeth's eyes and she covered her forehead with her hand. "But none of it is true! What if he believes it? I'm going to die. This is it. This is the end of my life."

"Liz, it's going to be okay."

"No, it's not!" Elizabeth blurted out, panicked. "This is insane. Caroline's out of her mind. She's making it all up. Why would she—"

Just then, Elizabeth and Jessica's red Jeep pulled into the driveway. Realization hit Elizabeth like a lightning bolt to the head. She might never have spoken to Rick Andover, but she knew someone who would have. Someone who looked just like her.

"Enid, I honestly don't know how this all got started, but I'm telling you, it's not true," Elizabeth said.

"I believe you, Liz," Enid said.

"Good. Thank you. I have to go, okay? I'll call you

back later." Without waiting for an answer, she hung up her cell and threw it on her bed. Down below, the front door slammed. Shaking with confusion and anger, Elizabeth headed for her door. She yanked it open just in time to see Jessica sprinting toward her.

"Omigod, Liz! I cannot believe this is happening!" Jessica cried, tearing past her into Elizabeth's room. "What are we going to do?"

"What are *we* going to do? *You're* going to tell everyone the *truth*!" Elizabeth fumed. "Starting with me!"

Jessica tossed her things down on Elizabeth's bed and turned to her. "What are you talking about?"

"The same thing you're talking about!" Elizabeth said, crossing her arms over her chest.

"So then you've heard too? How could Steven do this to us?" Jessica asked.

"Steven? What does Steven have to do with Rick Andover?"

"Rick Andover? Who cares about Rick Andover? I'm talking about our brother coming home every weekend and sneaking out to slum it with Betsy Martin."

Elizabeth felt as if the entire house had just spun her around like a Gravitron. "What!"

"That's who Steven's dating behind our backs!" Jessica

cried. "The girl's been arrested twice for drugs, and everyone knows her dad's an addict and a dealer. What the hell is Steven thinking?"

"Whoa, whoa, whoa. Back up. Where are you getting this information?" Elizabeth said. "And please do not tell me Caroline Pearce."

"That gossip? No way. Cara saw Steven going into Betsy's house last night when she was helping her mom with her Meals on Wheels thing. They had a delivery over there or something."

"Cara saw him?" Elizabeth said, dropping down on her settee. This was not good. The Martins were not the type of people she wanted her brother to get mixed up with. It was dangerous just being in their house, what with the kind of people who came around looking for a fix. Everyone knew that. Was Steven insane? Or worse— was he doing drugs himself?

Steven? Not possible, Elizabeth thought. But then why would he be hanging out at the Martins'?

"Yeah, and Cara's a solid source. She's one of my best friends, not some random gossip like Caroline Pearce," Jessica said.

Elizabeth brought her hands to her temples and squeezed her eyes shut. This was all just a little much for her to take. She took a deep breath and stared at her feet.

Her brother was on his way back to school right now, where he'd be safe and sound for at least a couple of days. For the moment, she could focus on that other small problem. The one that was systematically destroying her reputation.

"Okay, Jessica. Let's forget about Steven for a sec."

"Forget about him? Are you—"

"We'll deal with that in a minute. Right now I want to talk about Caroline Pearce, who apparently saw me getting dropped off by the police last night," Elizabeth said, lifting her head. "Any clue what that's all about?"

Jessica paled slightly. "Liz, our brother's life is at stake here. That's a little more important than—"

"This is important too," Elizabeth said. "What, exactly, was *I* doing out with Rick Andover last night?"

CHAPTER
8

ELIZABETH WAS BEYOND furious. Jessica could tell by the unattractive red blotches high on her cheekbones. Liz always went blotchy when she was really mad.

Quickly, Jessica considered her options. 1) Deny everything. But she had a feeling that Elizabeth had heard the whole story in too much detail for her to believe it was totally false. Damn that Caroline Pearce. 2) Burst into tears and beg for forgiveness. But since that approach always made her look weak, she only brought it out for really desperate occasions. 3) Tell the truth, but deny responsibility. As though she'd just been a little naïve. Gotten caught up in something she couldn't control. Which was basically the truth. Except that everyone knew that going out with Rick Andover was a dangerous proposition. Still, it could work. . . .

"Jess?"

"Liz, you have no idea how scary it was. But I didn't do anything wrong, I swear! I thought Rick was just going to take me out for dinner or something last night. I had no idea he was—"

"Wait a minute. I thought you were going out with Todd last night," Elizabeth said.

"Todd Wilkins? I wish!" Jessica told her, dropping down on Liz's bed. "Todd would never have treated me like that. And he'd never drive me around after he'd been drinking."

Liz's face drained of all color. "So that was true? You were drinking and driving?"

"Liz! No! I wasn't drinking, and I certainly wasn't driving Rick's car!" Jessica said. "How could you even think that about me?"

"Well, apparently the entire school thinks that about *me* right now." Elizabeth took a deep breath and crossed her arms over her chest. "Tell me exactly what happened."

"Okay. I went out to meet Rick, and instead of taking me somewhere normal, he drove me out to Coast Road and there were all these freaks there with their tricked-out cars. They were passing around bottles of something. So I told him right away that I did not want to be in the car with him if he was going to race," she lied. She hadn't protested until she'd realized how drunk he was. She knew she should've realized the moment he picked her up. She knew she shouldn't have gotten mixed up with him in the first place. And she knew her twin would point those facts out to her until they were beaten, dead, and buried.

"He wouldn't let me leave," she finished quietly. Jessica swallowed hard and her palms started to sweat. She still couldn't believe how close she'd come to . . . She didn't even want to think about that.

It's in the past. You're fine, she told herself.

"Omigod, Jessica. What did you do?"

"I tried to call you so you could come get me out of there, but he wouldn't let me. I was so scared, Liz," Jessica said, heaping it on—which wasn't that difficult, since it was true. "But luckily, that was when the police came and broke the whole thing up. I guess this kind of thing happens all the time, because the cops got me right out of there."

Elizabeth shook her head in disbelief. She sat down next to Jessica and put her arm around her. "I'm so glad you're all right."

Jessica leaned her head into her sister's shoulder, feeling triumphant. She had officially distracted her sister from the reason for her anger.

I am so good, she thought. *I should really write a book on this stuff. Or blog about it!* As if she was going to waste that much time sitting in front of a computer.

"But wait a minute," Elizabeth said suddenly.

Uh-oh, Jessica thought.

"None of that explains why Caroline thought it was me getting out of the car," Elizabeth said. "Enid said Caroline heard the policeman call you *Elizabeth.*"

"Oh, that," Jessica said with a dismissive laugh. She got up and went over to Elizabeth's dresser to toy with her jewelry box. "That was just his mistake. He was Emily Mayer's brother and he recognized you. Well, me. But he thought I was you."

"And you didn't correct him." Elizabeth's voice was hard.

"I tried to, Liz! But he wouldn't listen," Jessica lied. "You know how cops are. They're trained to be suspicious. He probably thought that I, as Liz, was trying to make him believe I was Jessica to get out of trouble. Besides, it was all a blur. I was just so happy to be home and safe I wasn't really thinking."

"Okay, fine. I get that. I do. But how did you go

through the entire school day today with all those stories floating around and not correct anybody?" Elizabeth demanded. "Everyone thinks I was arrested!"

I didn't correct anyone because then everyone would hate me, Jessica thought. Didn't Elizabeth get it? This kind of rumor wouldn't stick to pure-as-new-fallen-snow Elizabeth Wakefield, but Jessica was already known to be daring and up for anything. People might actually *believe* it about Jessica. She hated that fact, but it was a fact nonetheless.

"That's ridiculous, Liz. The cop just drove me home and gave me a warning. If I'd been arrested, they would have had to call Mom and Dad. I mean, how stupid can Caroline be?"

"Oh, so now it's Caroline's fault?" Liz said.

"Well, yeah! If she wasn't such a blabbermouth, no one would even know about this!" Jessica said. She still had no idea how Caroline had even seen her. If only Officer Mayer had brought her home five minutes later, or earlier, she might have gotten away with the whole thing.

"Please don't hate me, Liz," Jessica said. "Tomorrow I'll go into school and tell everyone it was me. I don't even care if no one ever talks to me again. Even though, you know, I might get thrown off the cheerleading squad for disgracing our image. . . ." She glanced over her shoulder at Liz to gauge her reaction. Luckily, her sister didn't jump at the offer. She wasn't kidding about the cheerleading squad. People had been cut for getting low grades. They wouldn't let rumored drinking go unpunished. The team had a certain image to maintain. All the athletes at Sweet Valley High were held to the same high standard. If you wore the red and white, you were on the straight and narrow. It was that simple. "But, you know, the rumor will probably just go away. Someone will do something stupid tomorrow and then everyone will be talking about that instead."

"I don't care about everyone, Jess," Elizabeth said, her shoulders slumping. "I just want my friends to know the truth."

"Yeah, but your real friends already know you'd never do something like that," Jessica said, sensing she was close to a full reprieve here. "Like Enid? You must've told her the truth. And she believes you, right?"

"Yeah." Elizabeth still looked depressed. Jessica narrowed her eyes. She had a feeling she knew who her sister was really worried about.

"Is there anyone else you want me to talk to for you?" she asked. "Todd Wilkins, maybe?"

Elizabeth blushed and looked down at her hands.

Jessica's heart skipped a beat. So it was true. Liz really did like Todd. Well, she was going to have to wait in line. Jessica had gotten there first. Once she set her sights on a guy, she did not give up. Not for anything. Not even for Liz.

"You two are, like, buddies, right? He's always saying what a good friend you are," Jessica lied. "Like one of the guys."

"He says that?" Elizabeth asked morosely.

"Sure! All the time!" Jessica trilled, as if this were a good thing. "Don't worry about Todd, Liz. I'll tell him the truth when he calls me later. He's been calling me pretty much every night lately."

"Oh," Elizabeth said. "Okay. Thanks, Jess."

"No problem, Liz!" Jessica said. "Consider it done." With that, she gathered her stuff and made her escape, leaving her sister catatonic behind her.

• • •

Enid sat on a blanket on the beach next to Ronnie, staring out at the water and wondering what, exactly, to say to him. During lunch they'd made a pact not to talk about Elizabeth anymore, since the subject clearly made them both so tense, but Enid couldn't stop thinking about it. Why was Ronnie so quick to judge Liz? Why couldn't he even consider the idea that Elizabeth might be innocent?

"Are you hungry?" Ronnie asked. "I could go for some ice cream."

"I'm fine," Enid said.

"Hey. Everything okay?" Ronnie asked, nudging her with his shoulder. "You're even quieter than usual."

Just do it, Enid told herself, clenching her fists. *Just ask him flat out.*

She turned to him and was about to open her mouth, when his eyes suddenly lit up.

"Wilkins! What's up, man?" he called out, pushing himself up. "Hope you don't mind, E. I told Todd we'd be out here."

Ronnie slapped hands with Todd, who had made his way across the beach with his surfboard. Enid pushed herself up as well, her heart pounding like crazy at the near miss. But she would talk to Ronnie about Liz later, she promised herself. Liz was her best friend.

"Hi, Todd," she said shyly.

"Hey, Enid. How's the water today?" he asked Ronnie.

"Kinda choppy," Ronnie said. "No good for surfing."

"Maybe I'll just go for a swim, then." He yanked his T-shirt off over his head, exposing his perfect abs.

"I was just gonna go for some food. You want anything?" Ronnie asked Todd.

"Nah," Todd said, looking down at the sand. "Thanks."

"Come on, dude. Cheer up," Ronnie said jovially, slapping Todd on the back. "She's just a chick."

Enid's heart lurched. Todd turned purple and glanced at her tentatively.

"Are you . . . are you talking about Liz?" she asked.

"I don't really want to talk about it," Todd said, averting his eyes.

"Bu—but it's not true," Enid blurted out with some effort. "She told me herself."

Todd looked at Enid hopefully, but Ronnie laughed. "Of course she denied it. What's she going to do, brag about it?"

"She wouldn't lie to me, Ronnie," Enid said, her skin heated to the point of burning. "She's my best friend."

Ronnie and Todd exchanged a dubious look, which just fueled Enid's frustration.

"Look, I know Liz, and she is not the type of person who's going to go out on a Tuesday night and fool around with a bunch of street racers." Enid laughed. "Actually, just the thought of it is hilarious. The girl does nothing but study and work on the Oracle and, like, clean her room. The rumor makes no sense."

"Well, sometimes people aren't what they seem to be," Ronnie said flatly.

Todd nodded. "Happens all the time. Besides, Caroline said she saw the whole thing."

"Well, Caroline says a lot of stuff," Enid said.

"So, what, Caroline's a liar now?" Ronnie demanded.

"Either she is or Elizabeth is. And I know who I'm voting for," Enid said. "And if you were her friend, you'd believe Liz. God! Even if she *did* do what everyone's saying, does that suddenly mean you can't be friends with her anymore? I mean, people do make mistakes."

Ronnie stared Enid down. "Yeah, but some things are unforgivable."

Enid choked on an air bubble that had appeared out of nowhere in her throat. How could he possibly be so stoic about this? Not everything in the world was so black-and-white. If Enid had learned anything in the past couple of years, it was that.

"So you're telling me that if she really was out there on Coast Road last night, there's no way you could ever forgive her," Enid said. "And I'm not saying she was. I'm just asking."

Todd took a deep breath and sighed, looking out at the waves. "I don't know. I really don't."

"Well, I do know," Ronnie said. "And if a girl I liked did something like that, that would be it for me."

"Really?" Enid asked.

"Really," Ronnie replied stubbornly.

"Fine. If that's the way you wanna be, I can't talk to you guys anymore." Tears prickled behind Enid's eyes, and she yanked her sweatshirt off over her head, exposing the basic black bathing suit beneath. "I'm going in."

Then she turned around and ran for the water, letting the tears flow silently as she dove into the waves.

CHAPTER
9

ELIZABETH WALKED INTO school on Monday morning with her head held high. Thursday and Friday had been much like Wednesday, with all the whispers and dirty looks, but after hiding out at home all weekend she had decided she couldn't be a hermit forever. She was going to face the gossip-hungry student body head-on. Let them say what they wanted to say about her. The people who really mattered knew the truth. She just hoped Todd Wilkins was one of those people.

Taking a deep breath, Elizabeth walked into the lobby of the school. The whole room was alive with chatter, and for a dreadful second, Elizabeth was certain they were all talking about her. But then she tuned in and realized that Jessica had been right all along. Something else had happened to make everyone forget about Liz and her questionable behavior.

"They can't do this," one of the football players said to his friends as Liz walked by. "That's *our* field."

"There's no way," Cara Walker protested. "We can't *not* have a football team. That's totally insane!"

Elizabeth's skin tingled with anticipation. Whatever was going on with the football field had finally become public knowledge. She had to know what was up. She grabbed Winston Egbert as he walked by, one of the few people who had still treated her like a normal human being last week. Winston's eyes widened behind his glasses when he saw who had grabbed him.

"God, Liz. Don't do that to a guy. Half the time when people grab my arm it's because they're about to kick my butt for no reason."

"Sorry, Winston. What's going on?" Elizabeth asked.

Winston glanced over his scrawny shoulder at the growing pack of football players. "Oh, that. Apparently Lila Fowler's dad is gonna turn the football field into a strip mall."

Liz gasped. "What?"

"No, no, no," Dana Larson said, joining them. Dana, lead singer of Valley of Death, was dressed, as always, in something black and baggy. Her dark hair fell over her heavily lined eyes as she leaned toward her classmates. "It's the Patmans. They're gonna build an amusement park out there. Which, let's face it, would be a much better use of the land."

"No doubt," Winston said. "That would rock! We could go on rides between classes. And think of all the corn dogs!" He turned around and took off down the hall, telling everyone he could find. "Dude! We're gonna have Disneyland in our backyard!"

Elizabeth laughed and rolled her eyes.

"Just so you know, Liz, I didn't believe any of that slop they were dishing last week," Dana said seriously, putting her hand on Elizabeth's shoulder. "Fight the power, girlfriend."

"Thanks, Dana," Elizabeth said, touched and amused. "I'm gonna go check in at the Oracle."

"Rock on," Dana said.

Elizabeth, of course, knew better than to trust any of the insane rumors buzzing around the lobby. She found Mr. Collins at his desk in the Oracle office, and he shot her a grim smile as she walked in.

"Mr. Collins, what's going on?" she asked. "You should hear the stuff they're saying out there."

"Oh, I have," he said. "And unfortunately, it's all true."

"I don't understand," Elizabeth said. "How could the Fowlers and the Patmans both be building on the football field?"

Mr. Collins stood up and squeezed the bridge of his nose between his thumb and finger. "Well, basically, the school leased the piece of land the football field sits on from the city about fifty years ago, and it seems no one's thought about it since. The current administration didn't even know that the field didn't technically belong to the school until last week, when the lease lapsed. The second that happened, both the Fowlers and the Patmans jumped on it."

"So, wait, the Fowlers want to build a strip mall on our field? What about the team?" Elizabeth asked.

"They don't care about the team," Mr. Collins responded. "All George Fowler cares about is making money."

"What about the Patmans?" she asked.

"Well, all the Patmans care about is not letting the Fowlers buy up the town," he said. "So they filed an injunction against the Fowlers and put in a bid for the plot as well. From what I understand, they want to plant an English garden over there. Something to commemorate the history of the land. Apparently back in the early nineteen hundreds it was part of the Vanderhorn estate."

"Who are the Vanderhorns?"

"They were one of the original families in Sweet Valley, and Bruce Patman's mother just happens to be one of them," he said. "It's all about old money versus new money, Liz. The Patmans against the Fowlers. It's like a bad Shakespeare play."

Elizabeth laughed and so did Mr. Collins. "What a mess," Liz said.

"Yes, it is. And it's all yours," Mr. Collins told her.

"Mine?" Elizabeth's pulse raced. She'd never had a story this big assigned to her.

"Yep. Normally I'd put Sports on it, but John is busy with the game against Palisades, if we ever get to play it. So it's all yours."

"Wait, we might not even get to play the first game of the season?" Liz asked.

"The Patmans' injunction keeps everyone off the land. As of right now, no one can use the field for anything."

"But the team has to practice somewhere," Elizabeth said.

"Well, apparently not on their own field," Mr. Collins said wryly. "Good luck with your story."

• • •

"I don't believe this! They cancelled practice!" Ken Matthews announced, shoving through the front doors and out onto the steps. Jessica and the rest of the crowd that had gathered after lunch to discuss the scandal all fell silent.

"What?" Jessica shook her head. "They can't do that."

"Apparently they can." Ken held out a crumpled piece of paper. "I just found this on the locker-room door."

Jessica quickly scanned the announcement as the rest of the crowd pressed in around her. "'Football and cheerleading practice suspended until further notice,'" she read. "This is insane. How are we supposed to get ready for the Palisades game?"

"We might not even play the Palisades game," Todd interjected. "Not unless they figure out this mess before then."

"Well, then they're just gonna have to," Cara said.

"Are you kidding? This kind of crap can take years to figure out," John Pfeiffer told them. "The football team is done."

"No," Ken said, his jaw clenched. "No way. Not when we finally have a shot. They can't do this to us!"

"Yeah!" Jessica exclaimed, her heart pounding with excitement. "That's our field. They can't take it away from us!"

The entire crowd cheered and Jessica beamed. This was the kind of moment she lived for—moments when she was the center of attention.

"We need a plan," Ken said. "We need to . . . I don't know . . . form a protest or something."

"What if we walk out?" Cara suggested.

"Walk out?" Jessica asked.

"Yeah, you know, that's what students do when they want to protest, right?" Cara said. "They stage a walkout. Cut class. As a group."

"Works for me," Ken said. "I have a geometry test this afternoon that I'd love to miss."

"All right then, a walkout," Jessica said. "Listen up, everybody! We're staging a walkout!"

Once again, she received a roar of approval.

"But, uh, Jess? It's lunch and we're already outside," Caroline Pearce pointed out.

Jessica gave her a sour look. As if Caroline hadn't caused enough problems lately.

"So then we don't go *back* to class, Caroline. Obviously," Jessica said snidely. Everyone within earshot laughed.

"And I say we go to the football field and take it back!" Todd suggested. "What're they gonna do? Bulldoze right over us?"

"Yeah!" a bunch of people shouted.

"Let's go!" Jessica announced, giddy at being in this whole thing right beside Todd.

He grinned at her. "Follow us!"

Jessica flashed a perfect smile and grabbed Todd's hand, leading the throng of cheering students across the street to seize Gladiator Field.

• • •

"Hey, everyone! Come on! It's a walkout!" Winston Egbert shouted from the door of the cafeteria. "We're taking over the football field."

Elizabeth dropped her sandwich and grabbed her digital recorder. She raced past Winston and got outside just in time to see her sister, Todd, and Ken Matthews stopping traffic to lead a huge crowd of students onto

Gladiator Field. She glanced up at the windows to the administrators' offices. Principal Cooper and Coach Schultz were standing right above her, clearly shouting at each other.

Liz hit the Record button and brought the microphone to her mouth as more students poured out the doors behind her.

"Principal Cooper and Coach Schultz watch helplessly as the captain of the football team and the captain of the cheerleading squad lead the student body protest. They are in clear disagreement about something. Make sure to get interviews later."

She jogged to catch up with the front of the crowd, pushing her way toward her sister and the rest of the cheerleaders. By the time she got to the field, half the crowd had cornered Lila Fowler and Bruce Patman by the bleachers. What they were even doing there, Elizabeth had no idea. If the two of them had any brains, they would have stayed in the library, hiding under a stack of books or something. She shoved her way into the circle and held out her recorder.

"What's up, Fowler? Your dad not rich enough yet?" Dana Larson demanded.

"Why do you even care, Dana?" Lila asked, grimacing as she looked the girl up and down. "You hate football."

"Yeah, but I hate imperialist social climbers even more," Dana said with a shrug.

"All George Fowler cares about is raking in the green, however dirty it is," Bruce said smugly. "If the Patmans get control of this property, it'll be a public garden for the whole town to enjoy."

"We don't want a garden. We want our field!" Ken shouted, earning a round of cheers.

"Yeah, Bruce. Where's your school spirit?" Jessica spat. "Don't you care about anybody but yourself?"

"Yeah. I care about my family," Bruce said.

"Well, your family's a disgrace," Jessica shot back.

"Look who's talking, Wakefield," Bruce retorted with a sneer.

Elizabeth swallowed hard as a few kids around her snickered.

Head high. Head high . . .

"What's that supposed to mean?" Jessica demanded.

"We all know what your perfect sister was up to last week—not that I disapprove of a girl who likes a little adventure." Bruce leered at Elizabeth, looking her over as if she were standing there naked. "But meanwhile, your father's running around with that hot young lawyer and your brother is slumming with the Martins. If anyone's family is a disgrace around here, it's yours."

Elizabeth felt as if she was going to throw up as laughter and murmurs abounded. But there was no way she could let Bruce talk about her family that way. "First of all, Bruce, my father is not running around with anyone. Marianna West works for my dad. In fact, they're working to stop *you*."

"Yeah, she works for him," Bruce said suggestively. "Or more accurately, *under* him."

Elizabeth felt as if she had been slapped. She looked at her sister, who was just about bursting with fury.

"Shut it, Patman!" Todd shouted suddenly, stepping out of the crowd. He turned and faced the throng, his back to Bruce. "We're not here to get personal. We're here to save the football field, remember?"

There was a halfhearted shout of approval from the crowd. Clearly, some people just wanted to hear more gossip. Still, Elizabeth couldn't have been more grateful to Todd for saving her.

"Are we going to let them take our field?" Todd shouted.

"No!" The response was much louder now.

"Are they building a strip mall here?" Ken asked, joining him.

"No!"

"Are they putting in a garden?"

"Hell no!"

"Who does this field belong to?" Ken cried.

"SVH! SVH! SVH!" the crowd chanted.

Elizabeth dove into the crowd, pulling people out for interviews and shouting details into her recorder to remember them better later. It was exhilarating, but there was a pain in her heart that would not fade anytime soon. She could handle people talking about her, because she knew that none of what they said was true. But her father . . . Hearing someone so far outside her circle talk about her dad and Marianna just made her suspicions feel all the more justified. Was Bruce right? Was it possible that her father and Marianna really were having an affair?

CHAPTER

10

IT TOOK ABOUT fifteen minutes for the Sweet Valley Police Department to arrive and strong-arm everyone into going back to school, promising that their protest was duly noted. Elizabeth asked one of the officers a few general questions before finally clicking her digital recorder off.

"Thanks, Officer," she said.

"No problem, miss. Now you'd better get inside before we start handing out official warnings," he replied.

"One more mark on your record, huh, Liz?" Bruce snickered as he walked by.

The officer looked at Elizabeth in confusion. *At least he doesn't know who I am. That means I don't have a crazy rep down at police headquarters,* Elizabeth thought. She blushed and turned away as quickly as possible, then walked right into Todd Wilkins.

"Hey, Liz," he said.

"Hi!" Suddenly, Elizabeth felt light as air. Just being around Todd could do that to her. It surprised her every time.

"Can you believe this?" he asked as they joined the crowd on its way back inside. "An actual protest at Sweet Valley High. I bet it's a first."

"Probably," Elizabeth said. "The town's not exactly known for its progressive politics."

"You covering it for the Oracle?" he asked, noticing her recorder.

"Yeah. It's my first big story," she replied proudly.

Todd smiled, and she felt prouder still. "Cool. That's . . . cool."

He paused and looked at the ground, serious all of a sudden. As if there was something he wanted to ask her. Elizabeth almost hoped he would bring up the Rick Andover debacle so she could set him straight. Not that she would tell him that Jessica had actually done, well, *some* of the things people were talking about. She wouldn't dish about her sister that way. But she wanted to clear the air with Todd and at least tell him she'd never met Rick Andover in her life.

"So . . . how are you?" he asked, pressing his hands together. "Is everything–"

"Todd! Liz! Wait up!" At that moment, Jessica came jogging over, all bright-eyed and flushed and gorgeous. She grabbed Todd's arm with both hands and grinned up at him. "We have *got* to talk," she said, tugging on his arm. "Got a sec?"

Todd glanced at Elizabeth. "Uh, sure," he said. "I guess I'll see you later?"

Elizabeth's mouth was suddenly dry as sand. She nodded mutely, then watched as her sister dragged away the love of her life.

It's fine, she told herself. *Just get to the Oracle and write your article. Writing always blocks out everything else.*

She joined the last of the crowd and headed into school.

● ● ●

"Todd! Hey, Todd. Focus!" Jessica said, snapping her fingers.

Todd stared after Elizabeth as if she were wearing a

thong bikini. Jessica rolled her eyes and grabbed both of Todd's arms. "Hello, rude! I'm trying to talk to you here," she said coyly.

Finally, Todd's eyes focused on her. "Sorry, Jess. It's just, do you think Liz is okay? She bailed kind of fast."

"Yeah, well—"

"She must be upset about what Bruce said back there," Todd said. "He's such a jerk."

"Tell me about it," Jessica said, her skin prickling with anger. Those things Bruce had said about Liz had really hit her where it hurt. Probably because he should have been saying them about *her*. "I don't understand why people can't just get over it already. What's the big freakin' deal?"

Todd looked at her, incredulous. "Well, it was kind of a big deal. Street racing with Rick Andover . . . drinking out on Coast Road and then getting behind the wheel . . ." Todd looked ill at the thought. "Getting arrested? God, sometimes when I think about it . . . it's like I don't even know her."

Jessica's fingers curled into fists. For the first time since the whole Rick Andover thing, she felt the real unfairness of it all. Things happened. People did things that seemed like they'd be fun at the time but turned into disasters. Like base jumping or swimming with sharks or, yeah, going out with Rick Andover. Who were all these people to judge her?

"Well, it wasn't her," Jessica said defiantly, shaking her hair back. She looked Todd directly in the eye and, in that moment, couldn't have cared less what he did next. "It was me, Todd. I'm the one who went out with Rick Andover. I'm the one who got brought home by the police. And what happened in between is nobody's business."

For a long moment, Todd gaped at Jessica. And for that same long moment, Jessica wished she could take back every single word.

He's going to walk away from me now. He's going to walk away and hate me forever.

But instead, much to her amazement, Todd laughed.

"Why are you laughing?" Jessica demanded angrily. "It's the truth. I'm sick of Elizabeth getting blamed for something I did. It was me, and I don't care who knows it."

Todd took a step toward Jessica, and for the first time since she'd spoken to him, truly looked into her eyes. He looked into them deeply, as if he was amazed by their beauty. Jessica's heart skipped a beat.

"You're unbelievable, you know that?" he said.

"What do you mean?" Jessica asked, breathless.

"Just . . . you know . . . that you'd try to take the blame for her," Todd explained. "That's just so . . . cool."

Suddenly, Jessica's elation turned into dread. "Todd, I'm not—"

"C'mere," he said.

Then he grabbed her hand and pulled her to him and Jessica lost all ability to speak. Todd slipped his hand around the back of her neck under her hair and leaned in to kiss her. Jessica's stomach swooped as his lips touched hers. She reached up to link her arms around his neck and hold him even closer. It was the most incredible kiss she'd ever experienced. Way better than those sour kisses with Rick. Better than anything.

"Go, Wilkins!" someone shouted, shattering the moment.

Jessica and Todd pulled apart and laughed, embarrassed. Still, he held on to her, slipping his hand down to the small of her back. Jessica was all tingles and butterflies.

"So . . . wanna go to the dance with me?" he asked, biting his lip adorably.

"Are you kidding?" Jessica asked, grinning back. Her

mind was fuzzy from the kiss, the triumph, the absolute perfection of the moment. "I'm totally there."

• • •

Elizabeth paused outside the Oracle office. This was ridiculous. She couldn't run away every time Jessica and Todd got near each other. If they weren't together, she'd just missed out on a potential opportunity to explain everything to Todd. And if they were together, she was going to have to get used to seeing them talk and hold hands and—oh God, kiss. It was time to be the bigger person here. It was time to swallow her feelings and just deal.

Taking a deep breath, Elizabeth turned around and walked back outside. Just in time to see Jessica and Todd coming out of a serious lip-lock.

"Oh my God," Elizabeth said, all her breath rushing right out of her. She raced back through the doors and into the lobby, where she tripped over the first step and went down hard, slamming her knee into the second. Tears filled her eyes and she bit them back.

"Liz! Hey, are you okay? That looked nasty!" Winston jogged down the stairs to pick up her books.

"I'm fine. Thanks," Elizabeth lied. She pushed herself up and sat down on the steps, taking in a nice, deep breath. Her knee throbbed, but it wasn't nearly as bad as the pain in her chest. She couldn't get the sight of Jessica and Todd kissing out of her head.

At least now you know for sure, she told herself. *Now you can stop obsessing about it.* Yeah, right. She knew now that seeing Jessica and Todd together was not something she would ever get used to.

"What happened here?" Bruce Patman asked, sidling over from the cafeteria. "Little Miss Fast Lane hit a speed bump?"

"Leave me alone," Elizabeth said through gritted teeth, mustering her best look of death, which she'd learned from Jessica. Although Liz's was still only about a tenth as effective as her twin's. She pulled herself up and took her books back from Winston.

Head high. Don't let him get to you, she told herself.

"You know what, Wakefield? You're not at all who I thought you were," Bruce said with a smile.

Elizabeth shook her hair back and eyed him with disdain. "I'm not sure if that's a good thing or a bad thing."

"Oh, it's good. Very good. So what do you think? You.

Me. Harvest Dance?" Bruce said. "We don't have to go for the whole thing. We can just make an appearance and then go—"

"I swear, Bruce, if you finish that sentence—"

"You'll what?" Bruce asked, amused.

Elizabeth clenched her jaw. She'd never felt so angry and sad and humiliated all at one time. But what was she going to do? Punch Bruce Patman in the face? An attractive image, but not likely. Next to her, Winston rolled from his toes to his heels and back again, over and over. Suddenly, Elizabeth knew exactly how to get back at Bruce. Hit him where it hurt. His too-large ego.

"You know what? It doesn't matter," Elizabeth said with a smile. "I already have a date."

"Oh yeah? With who?" Bruce said, still smirking.

"With Winston." Elizabeth turned to her friend, who immediately stopped rocking and let his jaw drop. "Right, Win?"

"Seriously?" Winston said.

"Seriously."

Winston slowly smiled, his face turning pleasantly pink. "It would be my honor to escort you," he said with a slight bow.

Elizabeth couldn't have been more grateful. She

slipped her arm around Winston's and smiled at Bruce. "Sorry, Bruce. You've been outmanned this time."

Bruce's eyes smoldered. "Wow, Liz. You're *really* not living up to your perfect reputation. First you're wild and now you're slumming. Hope you losers have tons of fun together."

He walked past the two of them and headed up the stairs, whacking Winston's forehead with the heel of his hand as he went.

"Ow," Winston whined, rubbing his head.

"Are you okay? What a jerk," Elizabeth said.

"I'm fine. Happens all the time," Winston told her. "So listen, I know you only said that to annoy him—which, brilliant maneuver, by the way—"

"Thank you," Elizabeth said, preening.

"So if you want to back out now, I totally understand," Winston said.

"I don't want to back out. Do you want to back out?" Elizabeth replied.

Winston's eyes widened. "Oh! No. No *way*."

Elizabeth laughed. "Winston, I can honestly say that at this moment, there is no one I'd rather go to the dance with besides you."

No one available, anyway, she added silently.

"Then I guess I'll . . . pick you up at seven," Winston said with a wide grin.

Elizabeth smiled back. "I'll be ready."

And hopefully we'll get out of there before Todd shows up for my sister.

CHAPTER
11

ELIZABETH SAW JESSICA waiting for her at the Jeep after school and her heart sank. Jessica was obviously bursting to tell Elizabeth her news. Liz could feel the heat from the girl's grin halfway across the parking lot.

Here goes nothing, Elizabeth thought.

"Hey, Jess," she said lightly.

Jessica pushed herself away from the Jeep. "Liz! You are never going to believe what happened."

"I might," Elizabeth said, opening the driver's-side door.

"I told Todd everything. I mean *everything.* I told him that it was me with Rick Andover that night and with the cops and everything and he *still* asked me to the dance!" Jessica exclaimed.

Not for the first time that day, Elizabeth felt sick to her stomach. "You told him?" she said, hazarding a glance at Jessica's ecstatic face. Which only made her feel more ill. "You told him it wasn't me?"

"Yes! Aren't you listening?" Jessica said impatiently. "I told him the whole story and he still likes me. He has got to be the coolest guy ever."

Jessica shook her head wistfully and walked around to the passenger side of the car without even trying for the keys.

Wow. She must be really *happy,* Elizabeth thought. She pulled her suddenly heavy body up into the car and fastened her seat belt. *Well, that's it, then. If he knows it wasn't me and he still likes Jessica . . . then that's really it.*

She wanted to smack herself for all those nights wasted dreaming about Todd. All those classes she'd only half paid attention to because she was busy staring at his earlobe or his hair or whatever part of him she could see from her particular angle. All those moments when she went completely giddy because she was sure he liked her back. What an idiot she had been. What a complete and total—

"Liz? Hello? Are we gonna go anytime soon?" Jessica snapped.

"Sorry," Elizabeth said. She started the engine and they were off. "What's the rush?"

"I want to get Mom to take me to the mall," Jessica said, checking her reflection in the vanity mirror. "There's this dress in the window of that new store that I'm dying to get. Todd won't be able to stop drooling all night."

Elizabeth's heart throbbed and she rolled her eyes at herself. "Jess, Mom's coming home late again, remember?" she said, stopping at a red light.

"What? Again?" Jessica blurted out. "I thought the whole point of her having her own business was that she could make her own hours. She always used to be home before we were."

"Yeah, but she's doing really well now," Elizabeth said. "More business means more time commitments."

"Oh, does it now, Miss Honor Student? Thanks. I couldn't figure that one out on my own."

Elizabeth stopped at another red light and stared at her sister. "What's the matter with you? Two seconds ago you were overjoyed and now all of a sudden you're freaking out."

"It's just, that dress is not going to be there

forever." Jessica sulked, scrunching down in her seat. "If Lila or Cara gets it before I do, I swear I'm never going to forgive Mom."

Elizabeth shook her head incredulously as the light turned green. How could Jessica possibly let something as stupid as a dress get her down on a day when Todd Wilkins had asked her to the dance? There was always another dress. There was only one Todd. And Jessica had gotten him.

If he'd asked me, I'd be so psyched I wouldn't be coming down for months, Elizabeth thought. *I wouldn't even care if I had a nice dress or not.*

She imagined herself and Todd dancing together in the center of the gym, the lights down low, a slow, romantic song filling the room. His arms around her. Her heart pounding. He'd look deeply into her eyes and ever so slowly lean in for a—

"Liz!"

"What?" Elizabeth cried, her heart in her throat.

"You just ran a red light!" Jessica shouted.

"What? No, I didn't," Elizabeth said, gripping the steering wheel.

"Well. It was yellow for a long time, anyway," Jessica grumbled.

"Sorry. I just spaced out there for a second."

Jessica rolled her eyes. "And they take *my* driving privileges away."

• • •

"Wait until you see this dress, Liz. It's blue and it's slinky, and—"

"Aren't you supposed to be setting the table?" Elizabeth asked, checking the chicken in the oven.

Jessica groaned and yanked open the silverware drawer. Sometimes her sister was just way too lame. But at least the store had agreed to put the last dress in her size on hold, which meant that now neither Lila nor Cara had a shot. All Jessica had to do was convince her mom to take her to the mall tomorrow and the dress was as good as hers.

"It has this asymmetrical hemline and these skinny little straps," Jessica continued, tossing two knives and two forks in the center of the table. "It's like it was made for my body. Todd will be seriously panting."

"Wow, Jess. You're really going for the kill with this one, huh?" Steven said, walking through the back door.

Jessica narrowed her eyes at him. "Do you even go to class anymore?"

"Like you're one to talk, Cut Queen," he joked back.

Jessica smiled. "Touché."

He walked over to check the oven. Then he peeked into the pot of rice and veggies Elizabeth was stirring on the stove. "Is there enough in there for one more? I'm starved."

"You're not going out?" Elizabeth asked in a leading way.

Steven cleared his throat. "Apparently not. Not tonight."

Jessica and Elizabeth exchanged a look. "Trouble in paradise?" Jessica asked.

"I don't want to talk about it," Steven replied, slipping out of his jacket. "What's up with you guys? Anything interesting going on around here?"

"Oh, just that the Patmans and the Fowlers are both trying to take away our football field, so there was a walkout today, which was broken up by the cops," Jessica said blithely. "Your average day in Sweet Valley."

"Wow," Steven said. "Can't leave this place for one day without missing out on a scandal."

"Yeah, well, you've come to the right house," Jessica told him, grabbing another set of silverware.

"What do you mean?" Steven asked.

"Well, in the middle of the protest, Bruce Patman

announced to the world that Dad is having an affair with Marianna West," Jessica told him.

"*What?*"

"Jess," Elizabeth said.

"What? He did, didn't he? Now everyone in the whole school knows about it."

"It's just rumors, Jessica. Just because Bruce shot his mouth off doesn't mean it's true," Elizabeth said.

"Fine, but Dad *has* been spending every single night working late with the woman," Jessica said.

"Right, and he *says* he's helping her with a case," Elizabeth put in.

"But you guys don't believe him?" Steven asked.

"How can we? Look at them. She's hot. He's hot—I mean, for a Dad. How could they *not* be having an affair?" Jessica said.

"They could *not* be having an affair because Dad wouldn't do that to Mom," Steven said, disgusted. "God, Jess. It's like you *want* to create drama."

Jessica felt as if she'd just been slapped. "You would defend him, Steven. Your taste in women is just as bad as his. Actually, worse."

"Jessica," Elizabeth scolded.

But Jessica ignored her. She was too busy glaring at Steven, who was glaring right back at her.

"What the *hell* is that supposed to mean?" Steven demanded.

"It means we know," Jessica said, taking a step toward him. "We know about you and *her*."

"Me and who?" Steven asked.

"We weren't spying on you or anything, Steve, we swear," Elizabeth said, stepping between the two of them. "Just, one of our friends saw you at her house."

"How did you even meet her?" Jessica said, repulsed. "The girl's in jail half the time and getting kicked out of school for fighting or passing out drugs in class the other half."

Steven took a deep breath. "Okay, now you've really lost me. Tricia isn't even *in* school right now."

Jessica and Elizabeth looked at each other, stunned.

"Tricia? You're going out with *Tricia* Martin?" Jessica said. "But she's totally . . . normal."

"Well, thanks for that vote of approval, Jessica," Steven said sarcastically.

"But she is still a Martin," Jessica reminded him.

Steven groaned and turned away. He actually banged his head once against the wall and stayed there.

And I'm *the dramatic one?* Jessica thought.

"Sorry, Steven. We didn't know," Elizabeth said. "I actually forgot all about Tricia."

"Of course you did. She *is* the only one in that family who isn't constantly in the police blotter," Jessica said.

"She was always so cool back when she was at Valley," Liz said. "We worked on the Oracle together and she was really nice."

"Yeah. She still is," Steven said mournfully.

"Then why do you sound so depressed?" Liz asked.

"Because she just dumped me," Steven said, turning away from the wall. "I wanted to take her out to a nice restaurant tonight because we never really get to go out, so I went over there to surprise her and she said she couldn't go and we had this huge fight."

"Why couldn't she go?" Liz asked.

"Well, her dad just got back from rehab and he's doing okay, like, mentally, but he's been really sick. He can't keep anything down and he's always dehydrated. So Tricia's been spending all her time at home taking care of him. We only ever hang out there," Steven said. "And I think it's cool that she's doing that for him. I really do. But I just thought she deserved a night off. I thought I was being a good boyfriend, you know? But she freaked out on me. She said I don't understand what she's dealing with and I never will."

Steven pulled out a chair from the kitchen table and flopped into it. "I don't know. Maybe she's right."

Jessica's heart went out to her brother. Even if he was sneaking around with someone from a seriously unsavory family, he didn't deserve to get his heart broken.

"I'm sure you guys will work it out, Steven," Elizabeth said, sitting next to him.

"Yeah. I'm sure you will too," Jessica told him. "If Todd Wilkins still likes me after everything I've done, then Tricia has to still like you after you made the *huge* mistake of trying to take her out for a nice date."

Steven and Elizabeth stared up at her as if she'd just said something completely stupid.

"What? Am I wrong?" she asked.

They both rolled their eyes and got up to finish making dinner. Jessica shrugged and headed off to make some phone calls. Sometimes she just did not get her brother and sister.

CHAPTER 12

"YOU ARE NOT going to the dance with Winston Egbert," Jessica said to Elizabeth on Thursday night, the night before the dance. She stood in the center of Elizabeth's room, hands out at her sides. "Liz! He puts the 'geek' in . . . 'geek.' "

Elizabeth laughed but didn't look up from her English notes. "That was very profound."

"I can't believe I'm only hearing about this now," Jessica said, pacing in front of Elizabeth's desk. "Why didn't you tell me when it happened?"

Because you were too busy gushing about Todd to care, Liz thought.

"I don't know. I guess I just didn't think it was important."

"Not important! If you'd told me then, I could have talked you out of it, but now it's too late!"

"Jess, he's my date, not yours," Elizabeth told her.

"Thank God for that."

Elizabeth sighed and finally looked up, leveling her sister with a glare. "Winston is a nice guy. He's my friend. And we're going to the dance as friends."

"Yeah, but don't you want a real date?" Jessica asked. "Somebody you could, I don't know, kiss goodnight without cracking up laughing?"

Yeah, that would have been nice. But you snagged the only guy I want to kiss goodnight, Elizabeth thought.

"No. I'd rather just have a good time," she said.

Jessica walked around Elizabeth's desk and sat down on the corner, right on top of the pages of a short story Elizabeth was writing. She gave Liz her best concerned-talk-show-host expression.

"Liz, are you going with Winston because you really want to, or because no one else asked you?" she said.

Elizabeth wanted to shove her sister right to the ground. But she had news that would hit Jessica even harder than a shove ever could. She pushed her notebook away and sat up.

"Actually," she said, looking Jessica right in the eye, "Bruce Patman asked me too."

"What?"

It was the screech heard round the world.

"Yep. Right before I asked Winston," Elizabeth replied.

"You did not turn down Bruce Patman." Jessica got up and squared off with Elizabeth in her chair. "How could you do that?"

"Well, it was pretty easy considering he'd just told half the school that our dad was a philandering jerk," Elizabeth pointed out.

Jessica paused, but not for long. "Yeah, but that's just Bruce. He's always been semiobnoxious."

"Semi?"

"But still, Liz, he's soooooo hot," Jessica said. "And I bet he'd take you to, like, Chez Louis or something beforehand. And that car. I mean, have you seen his car?"

"God, Jess. You'd think you'd rather go to the dance with Bruce than with Todd," Elizabeth said. She watched her sister closely for her reaction. Jessica quickly looked away.

"No. Of course not," she said. "Todd is, well . . . he's amazing."

"But not rich," Elizabeth pointed out, enjoying her little game. "And his car is kind of a junker."

Not that I care, but some people usually do. . . .

Jessica's brow creased in consternation. "That's true."

"And he's hot, but is he Bruce Patman hot?" Elizabeth said.

Even hotter, in my opinion, but in Jessica's . . .

"Well, no, but . . ."

Jessica crossed her arms over her chest and ruminated for a second. "Whatever, Todd's great. And we are going to have a great time," she said, sounding like she was trying to convince herself.

"Well, great!" Elizabeth said jovially.

"Great!" Jessica echoed.

"I really have to get back to my notes now, Jess," Elizabeth said. "I have a quiz tomorrow."

Jessica hesitated for a moment, as if she was confused, but then headed for the door. "Okay. Fine. I'll just go, then."

"Bye!"

Jessica closed Elizabeth's door with a bang and Liz hid a laugh behind her hand.

That was mean, she told herself.

But then again, it was also kind of fun.

• • •

Elizabeth watched out the window as Todd's car pulled up in front of her house. Of course he would get here first, when Jessica was miles away from ready. She, meanwhile, had been dressed and good to go for half an hour. Apparently, when it came to timing, she was far more compatible with Todd than Jessica was.

Todd got out of the car and smoothed the front of his sweater. Elizabeth's heart completely stopped beating. He looked gorgeous. All preppy, with his hair freshly trimmed, fiddling nervously with his keys. She didn't start breathing again until the doorbell rang. Then she ran to the stairs as if it were her date who had just arrived.

You're just torturing yourself, Elizabeth thought. But she wanted to hear his voice. She stood at the top of the stairs, just out of sight, as her mother answered the door.

"Hi, Mrs. Wakefield," he said. "I'm Todd Wilkins. I'm here for . . . uh . . . Jessica?"

Elizabeth felt a crack wend its way through her heart. She leaned her temple against the wall and tried to calm herself.

"Nice to meet you, Todd," Mrs. Wakefield said. "Come on in."

"Hi, Mrs. Wakefield!" Winston's voice piped up.

Elizabeth stood up straight. He must have pulled up right after Todd.

"Winston! Nice to see you again," Mrs. Wakefield said. She closed the door and called up the stairs. "Elizabeth! Jessica! The guys are here!"

Elizabeth took a deep breath and steeled herself. She walked carefully down the stairs in her new heeled sandals. The last thing she needed right now was to trip and fall in front of Todd. The first thing she saw as she descended was a pair of lightly scuffed black shoes. Then his legs in gray pants, then his hands in his pockets, and then . . . his face. His incredibly perfect, chiseled face and his warm brown eyes and his perfect mouth. Todd Wilkins was in her house. He was standing right there next to the planter Jessica had broken when she was twelve, the one Elizabeth had spent hours gluing back together. Todd Wilkins was right there . . . and he was staring at her.

For a long moment their eyes locked and Elizabeth could barely breathe. She could feel something change in the air between them. Was it possible that she'd been right all along? Could it be that he actually liked—

"Wow, Liz. Nice dress," Winston said.

Elizabeth looked at him for the first time. *Focus, girl. You have a date.* Recovering, she did a quick twirl, letting the full skirt of her white strapless dress dance around her. "You like?"

"I like," Winston said. He was wearing a button-down shirt and chinos, and his curly hair had been tamed by about a gallon of gel.

"Thanks. You look great too."

"Well, you know, after hours in the salon . . . ," Winston said, patting his hair.

Elizabeth laughed. "Hi, Todd," she said uncertainly.

"Hey, Liz. You look—"

"Hi, everyone!" Jessica trilled from the top of the stairs.

Ever so slowly, she descended in her sexy blue dress, her hair swept up, her makeup picture perfect. Elizabeth watched Todd as he watched her sister and felt a huge weight settle on her shoulders. She could see nothing different between the way he looked at Jessica and the way he'd looked at her.

"Hi, Jess. You look nice," Todd said, then cleared his throat. "Very . . . uh . . . ."

He turned beet red and Elizabeth found herself wishing she'd just grabbed Winston and run.

"Very pretty," he finished finally, glancing at Mrs. Wakefield.

It was almost imperceptible, but Elizabeth saw her sister's face drop for a split second. Jessica was disappointed. Disappointed that Todd had called her very pretty. What did she want the guy to do? Fall at her feet and declare his undying love?

Probably.

Elizabeth would have killed to have Todd tell her she was pretty.

"Well, I think you all look great," Mrs. Wakefield said, picking up her camera from the side table. "May I?"

"Uh, sure." Todd moved in front of the camera and was about to stand next to Elizabeth when Jessica squeezed her way in between them.

"Liz and I always have to stand together," she said.

Elizabeth forced a smile as her mom snapped the shot, her arm around Jessica on one side and Winston on the other. As soon as it was over, she grabbed Winston's wrist. "Come on, Win. Let's get out of here."

"Your wish is my command," Winston said, opening the door for her.

"See you guys there," Elizabeth said without a backward glance.

"Have fun!" her mother called.

"See ya, Liz!" Todd shouted.

Elizabeth jogged to Winston's waiting Jetta, forgetting all about her new heels. Nothing mattered at that moment except getting away from Todd and Jessica.

● ● ●

"Todd, this looks amazing," Jessica said, reaching for his hand as they walked into the gym. The place was all decked out in orange and yellow twinkle lights and thousands of autumnal-colored balloons. There were carved pumpkins everywhere, along with bales of hay, wheat stalks, and thousands and thousands of paper leaves. Jessica, of course, could have done something twenty times classier and more creative, but she'd had to lower her expectations since the football team had been in charge. "I can't believe a bunch of guys did this," she joked.

"Yeah, well, we worked pretty hard," he replied. He looked down at their entwined fingers as if he'd never seen his own hand before.

"Well, I hope to make tonight worth all the effort," she said, squeezing his hand and moving a little closer to him.

"Yeah. It should be fun," he said distractedly. His eyes scanned the room as if he was looking for someone more interesting to talk to. Jessica had to bite her tongue to keep from snapping at him.

You've got one of the most popular girls in school right here, you moron!

142

"Hey, there's Cara!" Jessica said, waving to her friend. Cara grinned and walked over. She was wearing a little black dress that was cute but seriously boring next to Jessica's outfit.

"Hey, Jess! Todd," Cara said, giving Jessica a hug. "You look gorgeous!"

"Thanks," Jessica said. At least someone had noticed.

"Omigod, you're never gonna believe who's dateless tonight," Cara said. "Bruce Patman!"

"Bruce came alone?" Todd said with a smirk. "Never thought I'd see the day."

"Yeah, well, that's what happens when a Wakefield turns you down," Jessica said with a shrug.

"No way. Bruce asked you? Why didn't you tell me?" Cara gushed.

"He didn't ask me. He asked Liz," Jessica said, glancing up at Todd.

"Bruce asked Liz?" Todd said.

"Well, why not?" Jessica said innocently. "*Tons* of guys asked her. She's got dates lined up till the end of the year."

Cara looked at Jessica quizzically, and Jessica shot her a look to keep her mouth shut. Luckily, Cara obliged. Todd, meanwhile, finally seemed to realize where he was and who he was with.

"Let's dance," he said, tugging on Jessica's hand.

"We just got here," Jessica fake-protested.

"It *is* a dance, isn't it?" he said.

Jessica laughed. "Can't argue with that logic."

The DJ was playing one of Jessica's favorite songs, and she immediately got into her own personal groove on the dance floor, just as she always did at any school function. Everyone knew Jessica was the best dancer in the junior class. What no one, including Jessica, knew until that moment was that Todd was almost as good. The boy had rhythm and zero self-consciousness, which already put him far ahead of the competition. Soon they were moving together as if they were made for each other, and everyone in the gym was watching them. Jessica, totally in her element, felt as light as air as Todd pulled her to him and moved to the music. As soon as the song ended, everyone cheered and Jessica threw her arms around Todd's neck, laughing happily.

Now, *this* was the date she'd been hoping for.

• • •

Elizabeth stared at Todd as her sister hugged him and laughed. Over Jessica's shoulder, Todd stared right back.

I wish that were me, Elizabeth thought, wondering if

144

Todd could read her expression. *I wish you were hugging me.*

"Hey, Liz! You want something to drink?" Winston asked.

As Jessica chatted with Cara and Lila on the dance floor, Todd just kept watching Elizabeth.

"Liz! Hello? It's me, Winston, your date-type person?"

Elizabeth finally snapped to when Winston raised a plastic cup full of soda in front of her face. "Oh, sorry, Winston. What were you saying?"

"Can't take your eyes off Wilkins, huh?" Winston said affably, shaking his head. "How the heck did that guy get both the Wakefield twins to fall in love with him?"

"It's that obvious?" Elizabeth asked, sick of keeping everything to herself.

"You may as well have the word 'gaga' stamped across your forehead," Winston joked, taking a sip of his drink.

Liz backhanded his arm but laughed. "Well, you've been looking at my sister the same way since kindergarten," she teased.

Winston sighed and gazed across the gym at Jessica. "It's true. Too bad she's never once looked at me."

They both stared wistfully at their crushes as Todd and Jessica came together for a slow dance. "Well. This is depressing," Elizabeth said finally. Out of the corner of her eye she noticed Enid waving at her. "Let's go talk to Enid. I haven't seen her all night."

"I'm in. But good luck getting Enid alone," Winston said, putting his cup down. "I haven't seen Edwards leave her side in about a week."

"He is kind of protective, isn't he?" Elizabeth said as they moved through the crowd.

"Yeah. Like a Doberman," Winston said under his breath.

• • •

Jessica sighed happily, lifting her head from Todd's shoulder. She looked up at his cheekbone and . . .

Hang on. That's not right.

"Todd?"

"Yeah?"

Perturbed, Jessica followed his gaze. Elizabeth. He was watching her sister weave through the crowd toward that dork Enid Rollins and her robot boyfriend, Ronnie, with Winston Egbert tripping at her heels. The very company Liz chose to keep should have turned Todd right off, but no. He was riveted. Un. Be. Lievable.

"Todd!" Jessica said, snapping her fingers in front of his face.

"What? Oh. Sorry, Jessica." He looked at her for the first time in several minutes. The girl he currently had his arms around. As if he'd just remembered she existed. "What'd you say?"

Jessica narrowed her eyes at him. "Nothing. Forget it. I'm gonna go get something to drink."

He dropped his arms. Just like that. "Okay. Want me to come with you?"

"No. That's fine," she said. "Why don't you go see what Elizabeth and Enid are talking about? From the look on your face you're dying to know."

Todd blushed slightly and Jessica brushed by him, heading for the snack table and a few friends gathered there. If that didn't wake Todd up to his rude behavior—if there wasn't a complete turnaround by the time she got back—then she was just going to have to take drastic measures. Guys didn't look at other girls when they were out with Jessica Wakefield. It simply was not done.

• • •

"I'll walk you to the door," Todd said, getting out of his car.

You bet you will, Jessica thought. It was the least he could do after being half out of it all night. About the only time he had acted normal was when they had gone out after the dance to Casa del Sol with the rest of their friends. He'd laughed, put his arm around her, made sure she had enough to drink. It had actually felt like a date. But Jessica had the unfortunate feeling that it had only happened because Elizabeth had gone straight home—she'd no longer been there to gape at.

She got out of the car and walked side by side with Todd up the front walk. *Okay, if he kisses me goodnight, I'll forgive him. If he kisses me at all like he did that day at school, he's all mine.*

They paused under the light over the front step and faced one another.

"So . . . ," Todd said.

"So."

Jessica's heart pounded an insane beat, remembering that kiss.

"I had fun," Todd said.

"Me too," Jessica lied.

"Well . . . thanks," Todd told her.

Then, just as her eyes were fluttering closed for that kiss, he turned and jogged down the steps.

"Thanks?" she repeated, horrified.

Todd paused and turned, still backing toward his car.

He lifted his hand to scratch the back of his neck. "Yeah, thanks. It was great," he hedged. "I'll . . . see you in school!"

And two seconds later, he was gone.

"You have *got* to be kidding me," Jessica said. She looked down at her cleavage-baring dress. At her smooth, tan, gorgeous legs. At the perfection that was herself. This didn't even get a tiny little kiss?

"Oh, you are so done, Todd Wilkins," Jessica said through her teeth, shaking as she tried to shove her key into the lock. "So very, *very* done."

● ● ●

Elizabeth quickly turned off her bedside lamp and snuggled down into her bed, pretending to be asleep. She did not want to know what Jessica and Todd had done on the front step. She did not want to know what they'd done in the car. She didn't even want to know what they'd eaten at Casa del Sol. All she wanted to do was to forget this night had ever happened.

The door to Elizabeth's room flew open. "Oh my God, Liz!"

Apparently, she and Jessica were not on the same page.

"Jess?" Liz yawned and faked grogginess. "What time is it?"

"Who cares? Liz, I have to talk to you."

Suddenly, Elizabeth was fully alert. Was Jessica crying?

"What's wrong?" Elizabeth turned on the light, and sure enough, there were mascara tears running down Jessica's face. "Oh my God, Jess. What happened?"

"Todd Wilkins happened," Jessica said, dropping down on Elizabeth's bed. She flung her arms around Elizabeth, and for the briefest of seconds, Elizabeth felt a flicker of hope. Had Todd dumped Jessica?

Okay. You're evil. She's your sister, Liz. Wake up.

"Did he . . . did he break up with you?" Elizabeth asked, pulling back.

"I wish," Jessica wiped under her nose with her hand. "He practically raped me."

"What?" Elizabeth shouted, fear gripping her entire body.

"Well, I mean, he didn't *rape* me," Jessica said. "But he tried just about everything else. No matter how many times I told him to stop or that I wanted to go home. He was just . . . he was all over me."

Elizabeth's mind could not wrap itself around this information. There was just no way she could ever picture

Todd attacking her sister like that. "Jess, come on. Really. Todd?"

"You don't believe me?" Jessica was horrified. "Why would I lie about something like that?"

"I don't . . . I don't know," Elizabeth said. "It's just Todd is so . . ."

"Nice. I know," Jessica said sarcastically. "Well, apparently it's all just an act. Instead of taking me home after Casa, he drove me to the park, and I was all, *Cool*. I mean, I like to make out with a hot guy as much as the next girl—"

Elizabeth swallowed hard and tried to concentrate.

"And it was fine for a little while, but then all of a sudden he was shoving his hand, like, under my bra and trying to go up my dress and he didn't even . . . he didn't even, like, ask me if it was okay or *anything*. He was just everywhere!"

Elizabeth felt dizzy. Dizzy and beyond confused. "How did you . . . how did you stop him?" she asked, her throat dry.

"I finally shoved him off me with both hands and told him if he didn't drive me home I was walking," Jessica said. "That was when he called me a prude and got all pissed off. He didn't say one more word to me the whole way home. I guess I should be happy he even bothered to drive me."

"I think I'm gonna throw up," Elizabeth said, bringing her hands to her head.

"Maybe when I told him it was me and not you out on Coast Road with Rick Andover, he figured I was up for anything. I bet that's why he really asked me to the dance."

Jessica dissolved into tears and Elizabeth felt her blood run cold. Was Jessica right? Had Todd really only asked her out because he thought she was some kind of slut?

"I just can't believe Todd—"

"What's so hard to believe, Liz? He *is* still a guy," Jessica said, grabbing a tissue and blowing her nose. "And we all know that guys only want one thing, right?"

Elizabeth swallowed a lump in her throat. Todd Wilkins. Sweet, funny, beautiful Todd Wilkins. The guy she'd been daydreaming about ever since the first day of school. Todd Wilkins was actually a womanizing jerk?

"I don't believe this," Elizabeth said again.

"Fine. Don't believe me. Whatever." Jessica started to get up, but Elizabeth grabbed her hand.

"No. It's not that I don't believe *you*, it's just . . . I don't know what else to say." She looked up into her sister's sad eyes. "Are you okay?"

Jessica nodded mournfully. "Yeah. I'll be fine."

"Good," Elizabeth said. She pulled Jessica down and hugged her for real. "I'm so sorry this happened to you, Jessica. I'm just so sorry."

"I hate him, Liz," Jessica said, sniffling. "I hate him *so* much."

"So do I," Elizabeth said, her hands clenching into fists. "Believe me. So do I."

CHAPTER
13

STEVEN TROMPED DOWN the stairs just after noon on Saturday, his grumbling stomach forcing him out of his room and toward the kitchen. It was, as usual, a gorgeous sunny day out—a fact he wished he could ignore. All he wanted to do was get one of the huge salad bowls out of the cabinet, fill it with Froot Loops and milk, and go back up to his cave of a room, where the blinds were down, the lights were out, and there were four college football games on TV, none of which he needed to pay attention to. But when he walked into the kitchen, both of his parents were standing there, as if they had anticipated the exact moment his hunger would win out over his depression.

"Good morning, Steven. Or should I say good afternoon?" Mrs. Wakefield said.

"Hey."

Steven walked past her in his boxer shorts and T-shirt and went for that bowl.

"So, the girls told us about you and Tricia Martin," she said.

Steven's shoulders slumped and the bowl in his hand banged into the table. "Of course they did."

"Don't take that tone, Steven. They're just worried about you," his father told him.

"Well, they found out on Monday. I guess I should be impressed that they held out almost a week," Steven said.

"What I don't get is why you felt you had to keep it from us," his mother weighed in, reaching for the coffeepot. "Tricia's a lovely girl."

"Yeah, well, it doesn't matter anymore anyway," Steven said. "She broke up with me Monday."

"Well, from what it sounds like, you didn't exactly fight her on it," Mr. Wakefield said.

Steven sighed and turned around, leaning back

against the counter. His heart felt like some superhero was squeezing it in his superstrong fist. "Do you think I should have?"

"If you care so much about her that you're sleeping till noon and walking around looking like that, then I'd say yes," Mrs. Wakefield replied. She took a sip of her coffee, her blue eyes dancing above the rim of her mug.

"Way to kick me when I'm down," Steve joked back halfheartedly.

"So what stopped you?" his father asked.

Steven's standoff with Tricia suddenly came back at him full force, and he shook his head. "I don't really feel like talking about this with you guys." He grabbed the box of cereal and headed for the fridge.

"Why? You think we never had problems in our love lives?" Mr. Wakefield asked.

According to the twins, you're having one right now, Steven thought. But this hardly seemed like the time to open up that can of worms.

"No, it's just . . . I don't know," Steven said with a shrug. "I guess . . . no . . . I didn't really fight for her, and if you want to know why, I guess it's just . . . it's all so complicated, you know? I mean, we always have to be at her house with her dad, which is kind of depressing. And then her sister's always stressing her out . . . coming home late, doing God knows what with God knows who. It's just really . . ."

"Messy?" his mother said.

Steven deflated under his parents' admonishing gaze. "I sound really shallow, don't I?"

"No, Steven. You don't," Mrs. Wakefield said. She put her coffee cup down and placed her hands on his shoulders. "There's nothing wrong with wanting your relationship to be light and fun. You're only nineteen. It's natural to want those things."

Steven nodded, averting his gaze.

"But if you love her, then you should be there for her," she continued. "It sounds like Tricia's life is pretty stressful and kind of lonely. I'm sure all she wants is to feel like someone really cares. Like someone will stick around and not . . ."

"Not give up so easily, like I did?" Steven said, feeling ill.

"It's just a thought," his mother said with a sympathetic smile.

Steven turned and put the box and bowl down on the table. He collapsed into a chair and leaned back, staring at nothing. "Wow. I really suck."

"I wouldn't say that, kiddo," his father said, patting him on the back as he sat down at the table. "You're just learning as you go along. That's what we're all do-ing," he added, smiling up at his wife. "The key is to actually learn, and not just keep making all the same mistakes."

Steven nodded, letting all this sink in. He wondered if Tricia would even talk to him if he called over there. If she would even let him apologize. But just the thought of trying—just the thought of seeing her—made him feel more awake and excited than he'd felt in days. He knew what he had to do.

"So what's it gonna be?" his father asked.

"I'm going over there, and I'm going to apologize," Steven said, shoving back from the table. "Even if she slams the door in my face. Then I'll just . . . apologize through the window."

"There you go!" Mr. Wakefield said.

"Thanks, you guys." Steven beamed at his parents. "I'll let you know how it goes."

He turned around and headed for the front door, grabbing his keys on the way.

"Uh, Steven! You might want to get dressed first!" his mother shouted after him.

Steve paused and looked down at his boxers, his knobby knees, his mismatched socks. "Thanks, Mom!" And he took a quick detour upstairs.

• • •

Steven shifted from foot to foot on the tattered welcome mat outside Tricia's front door. He'd knocked quietly at first, not wanting to wake her father if he was napping, but no one had responded. So he'd knocked harder. Still nothing. He was starting to wonder if Tricia had seen him coming and decided to hide out in her bedroom, when the door finally opened.

He almost gasped at the sight of her. Her auburn hair was pulled back in a ponytail, and she wore a light blue T-shirt that brought out her eyes. She was one of the only girls Steven had ever known who could get his heart pounding just wearing a T-shirt and jeans.

Unfortunately, she kept the screen door closed and stared at him through the crisscross pattern.

"Steven. What're you doing here?" she asked.

"I just wanted to say I'm sorry. I was an idiot the other night," Steven said. "I should have checked with you before I made plans. I mean, I know you have more responsibilities than a lot of other people, and I should have been, you know, respectful of that, and I wasn't."

Tricia's expression softened slightly, and Steven felt a surge of hope inside his chest.

"The thing that's really stupid is, I love that you care so much about your family. It's one of the things I love most about you. And that night I made it sound like I felt the exact opposite," Steven said. "So I'm really sorry, Tricia. And it won't happen again. I mean, if you'll give me a second chance."

She looked down at her feet and didn't say a word. Steven held his breath. Had he said too much? Was there something wrong in there? But when Tricia looked up again after a long moment, she was smiling. There were tears in her eyes, but she was smiling. Steven's heart leapt.

"That was good?" Steven asked.

Tricia nodded and wiped a tear from her face. "That was really good."

She pushed the door open, and Steven grabbed her in his arms. A huge wave of relief washed over him. It was like coming home.

"I missed you *so* much," he said.

"I missed you too," she replied. "And hey! Guess what? My dad felt a little better this morning and went out to an AA meeting, so I . . . am free!" she announced happily.

"Well then. Let's go do something. Anything you

want," Steven told her. Then his stomach grumbled audibly and Tricia laughed.

"Food, then?" she asked, grabbing her purse.

"Food is good," Steven replied. "But wait just one sec." He took her hand, stopping her on the way out the door, and when she turned her face to his, he kissed her as if he'd never kissed anyone before. As if he was in love. As if he was never going to let her go.

● ● ●

That night, Steven drove home after hanging out with a few of his old high school friends, feeling light enough to float. He'd spent an incredible afternoon with Tricia, talking and laughing over tacos at Casa del Sol, and when he'd brought her home the house had still been empty, so they'd even had a chance for some private make-up smooching. Then his buddy Jason had called and said a few of the guys were home for the weekend and were coming over to play poker. Steven had gone and he'd cleaned up. All in all, the day that had started out miserable had completely turned itself around.

Steven was just turning onto Peach Street when he saw his father's Audi up ahead. It looked as if he was heading home from somewhere as well. But a couple of blocks later, his dad made a right turn, away from Calico Drive. Without thinking much about it, Steven turned the wheel and followed.

"Okay. Interesting decision," Steven said to himself. What was he doing, spying on his dad? But he told himself that if his father was running an errand or something, he could help out when they got wherever they were going. His dad would laugh and be grateful to have someone there to help him carry the . . . whatever he was buying. Yeah. That was it.

Mr. Wakefield took another turn, and Steven saw for the first time that there was someone in the car with him. A petite someone with dark curly hair. Definitely *not* Mrs. Wakefield.

Oh God. Was this the infamous Marianna West he'd heard so much about? She fit Jessica's detailed description. What was his father doing out with this woman on a Saturday night?

Steven sat up in his seat and gripped the steering wheel. He could admit it now—he was spying. But it was for a good cause. He had to find out what was really going on between these two.

Suddenly, his father slowed. Steven did the same, hanging back a little. He checked his rearview mirror.

Luckily, there was no one behind him. Mr. Wakefield pulled into a random driveway. Steven slid up to the curb a few houses away and parked, killing his headlights.

Mr. Wakefield and Marianna got out of the car. He said something. She laughed, tossing her hair over her shoulder. Mr. Wakefield placed his hand on the small of her back and escorted her into the house. Her house, Steven figured. His father and this woman alone in her house on a Saturday night. His heart clenched and he sank down in his seat. This did not look good.

Okay, maybe he's just dropping her off after some client dinner, Steven thought. *Maybe he'll come right back out.*

He turned on the radio to distract himself and waited. And waited. One song ended. A second song ended. Three. Five. Eight. Commercials. Steven thought about walking up there and pounding on the door. Demanding to know what was going on. But he was more scared to know than he was scared of doing nothing. Finally, feeling like a complete wuss, he turned the engine on and drove home.

CHAPTER
14

ELIZABETH GLARED AT the back of Todd's head through-out history class. She couldn't believe she had ever liked a guy like him. He'd had her completely snowed. She looked at that perfect hair. Not one strand out of place. And those shoulders. Those annoyingly broad shoul-ders. Every day he walked around SVH like Mr. Perfect, when really, inside, he was completely disgusting. It made her want to hurl something at him. Something heavy.

The bell rang and Elizabeth shot out of her chair like she did after every class she shared with Todd these days. He got up and turned right around to talk to her, but she dodged into the next row, nearly tripped over Dana Larson's book bag, and careened through the door.

"Liz! Wait up!" Todd called after her.

Why did he want to talk to her? This had happened almost every day this week. Did he think she didn't know what he'd done? Did he think that she and her sister didn't talk about these things? Maybe he was a clueless moron on top of everything else.

Elizabeth was just about to shove through the door to the stairwell when Todd caught up to her. He had annoyingly long legs.

"Okay, what is going on?" Todd asked her.

"Nothing," Elizabeth replied, starting up the stairs.

"Well, obviously something's going on. You've been avoiding me for two weeks," he said.

Huh. He was keeping track? Weird.

"I don't know why I would be doing that," Liz said sarcastically.

He held the door open for her at the top of the stairs. Just another affectation of his perfect in-school persona.

"Liz, come on. I really want to talk to you," he said.

"Yeah, okay. This I have to hear. Go ahead. Talk."

She stopped in the middle of the hallway, forcing all the traffic to part around her. Todd pushed his hand into the pocket of his jeans and looked around warily.

"Not here," he said, clearly uncomfortable. "Meet me after school? By the benches out front?"

He had to be out of his mind. Why would she ever make plans to chat with the guy who basically attacked her sister? But he looked so desperate it gave her pause. Was there some explanation for what had happened? Some detail Jessica had left out?

No. There was no way to explain what he'd done. He was a jerk, plain and simple.

"Please, Liz."

Elizabeth rolled her eyes. "Whatever." Then she turned and shoved through the mayhem.

"Was that a yes?" he called after her.

She didn't bother to answer. Instead, she opened the door to the Oracle office and let it slam behind her. Mr. Collins looked up from his desk, startled.

"That was an entrance," he said.

"Sorry," Elizabeth replied, her shoulders slumping so fast her bag strap slid off her shoulder and the whole thing hit the floor. They both stared at it. "Bad day."

"Well, I don't know if this is going to make it better or worse, but the hearing about the football field is going to start tomorrow afternoon," Mr. Collins said. "You up to covering it?"

Going to court to watch my father and Marianna West work

side by side? Sounds way fun, Elizabeth thought. But this was her job. She knew she couldn't let her personal issues get in the way.

"Sure, Mr. C," she said.

"I know your dad's working on the case. You're going to have to do your best to remain objective," he told her.

Like anyone at this school could be objective about potentially losing our football field—especially just when the team was getting good, thanks to Ken and Todd. Ugh.

"I will. Don't worry."

He wrote something down on a slip of paper and handed it to her. "That's the designated courtroom and the time the hearing is scheduled to start. You might want to get there early to get interviews with the key players."

"I'm there," Elizabeth said, pocketing the info. Maybe she'd even interview Marianna West, and her first question would be "Are you or are you not fooling around with my father?"

"Good luck," Mr. Collins said with a smile.

"Thanks."

I am so *going to need it,* she thought.

• • •

That night Elizabeth was typing up some questions for her story when her cell phone rang. It was an unrecognized number. Figuring it might be one of the people she had contacted about the case, she hit Talk and answered.

"Hello?"

"Liz? It's Todd."

Elizabeth's heart automatically skipped a beat, then lurched. How could his voice still get her all excited after everything that had happened?

"Todd! What—"

"You weren't there."

He sounded angry. Elizabeth suddenly felt an intense need to move. She got up and paced in front of her desk.

"I wasn't where?" she asked.

"At the benches. After school? I waited for an hour."

Elizabeth's eyes narrowed. The unbelievable gall . . . "I don't think I actually said I was going to be there," she pointed out.

"Fine. Whatever," he said. "If you don't want to hear me out, then—"

"Hear you out?" Elizabeth snapped. Did he really think there was something he could say that would make what he'd done all right?

"Yes!" Todd replied, frustrated.

Elizabeth sat down on the edge of her bed, clutching the phone. She crossed her legs and held herself around her waist with her free hand, every muscle in her body tight.

"You know what, Todd? Go ahead. I'm dying to know what you have to say."

There was a long pause and a sigh. "I don't know why you're being so—"

"I'm waiting," Elizabeth interrupted.

"Fine. What I wanted to say was . . . people make mistakes. We all know that, right? I mean, we all make mistakes. Some are bigger than others, yeah, but it happens every day."

Elizabeth's brow knitted. What the heck was he babbling about? Was he going to chalk up his treatment of her sister to a harmless mistake?

"And I figure if someone messes up, it's stupid to hold it against them forever," Todd said. "Especially if you . . . you know . . . care about them."

Annoyingly, Elizabeth's heart skipped another beat. She rolled her eyes at herself and gripped her sweater tighter.

"Anyway, the point is, I wanted to apologize for how I acted when it all happened. I think I was unnecessarily cold to you and I'm sorry. That wasn't right."

Elizabeth looked around the room as if something there could explain that total non sequitur. "Wait. *You* were cold to *me*? When what happened, exactly?"

"You know. After you and Rick Andover—"

"What? That's what you're talking about?" Elizabeth was on her feet.

"Well, yeah. What did you think I was talking about?" Todd asked.

"Oh. My. God. You have *got* to be kidding me," Elizabeth said, pacing the room again. She could not believe this. She could not believe that after the way he had behaved, he was calling to benevolently forgive *her* for her *supposed* behavior. "First of all, the fact that you ever believed that I would do something like that makes me so, so . . . there isn't even a word. And secondly, Jessica *explained* it to you! She told you it was her and not me out there!"

"Liz. Come on. We both know she took the bullet for you," Todd said with a scoff. "Don't act like we both don't know what really happened."

Elizabeth covered her forehead with her hand. "You are just . . . just . . ." She sputtered, searching for any word she could use that would make him understand just how frustrated she was at that very moment.

"You know what, Todd? Don't ever call me again!" she

shouted. Then she hung up the phone, turned it off, and hurled it down on her bed, where it bounced off and smacked against the wall.

"Psycho!" she shouted at the top of her lungs.

That was it. That was really, *really* it. Elizabeth Wakefield was done with Todd Wilkins. Forever.

CHAPTER

15

STEPPING INTO THE airy, marble-walled foyer of the Sweet Valley courthouse, Elizabeth suddenly felt nervous and very out of her league. Throughout the room adults in stylishly cut suits chatted on their cell phones and texted away on BlackBerries. Elizabeth's digital recorder and spiral reporter's notebook felt like a child's toys in her hands.

You're fine. You're here to do a job, so just . . . suck it up.

She walked over to one of the guards near the doorway, her sensible shoes clip-clopping on the shiny floor.

"Excuse me? I'm here to cover the Sweet Valley High

football field case?" she said, her voice squeaky. She fished out the press pass Mr. Collins had procured for her and flashed it, feeling as if she were trying to fake her way into a club.

"Yes, young lady. Right down the hall," the elderly gentleman said, pointing over her shoulder. "The press room is the third door on the left."

"Thank you." Elizabeth smiled.

The press room. How very official. She was feeling better already. After making it through the metal detectors, Elizabeth found the designated room, which was really just a balcony overlooking the courtroom. There were about two dozen chairs, most of which were filled. She found a seat near the back and took out her recorder, smiling politely at the other reporters, who gabbed around her.

Down below, the judge was already seated at his bench, his white hair combed back from his face and his glasses on the tip of his nose. There were three tables set up in front of him. At the first was Lila's dad, George Fowler, tanned and athletic, looking handsome and foreboding in his dark suit. At the second was Bruce Patman's dad, Henry Patman, who had a bit of a paunch and graying hair but was nonetheless dignified. At the third table were Coach Schultz, Principal Cooper, and the two people Elizabeth had been dreading seeing all day long—her father and Marianna West. They were sitting next to each other, whispering.

Elizabeth felt an icy stab of anger go through her. If her mother saw this, she would lose it.

Objectivity, Liz. Pretend you don't even know them. What would you see if they were just two people you'd never met?

Marianna's laughter suddenly filled the courtroom and she put her hand briefly on Mr. Wakefield's arm.

Yeah. I'd see two people flirting shamelessly in front of the entire town.

Luckily, at that moment, the judge called the room to order and everyone got down to business. Elizabeth turned her recorder on and sat forward to take notes.

First, one of Mr. Fowler's lawyers got up and delivered a long speech about how the Fowlers were entitled to the football field property because the lease held by the Sweet Valley Board of Education had lapsed and had not been renewed. The Fowlers had made a generous offer for the land before anyone else, so the property should be sold to them.

Then one of Mr. Patman's lawyers delivered an even longer speech about how the town didn't need another strip mall and how the Patmans' plan would beautify the town rather than deface it. Plus, their offer had been even *more* generous.

Much to her chagrin, Elizabeth found herself agreeing with both of the lawyers. Their arguments sounded very astute and made total sense. Which, she supposed, was why they got paid the big bucks. Their job was to win people over, and they were both very good at their jobs.

Still, her father hadn't had his chance yet. He was good at his job too. Maybe he could still save the field for Sweet Valley High.

"Thank you, Mr. Lawrence," the judge said when the Patmans' lawyer was done. "Now we'll hear what the school board has to say."

Go, Dad! Liz thought, sitting on the edge of her seat.

But her father didn't move. Instead, Marianna West stood up and walked to the front of the table. In the public gallery, Elizabeth saw Ken Matthews and a couple of other guys from school—including Todd—shift and whisper appreciatively. Even her classmates thought Marianna was a babe. *So* not good.

"Your Honor, I submit that taking the football field away from the students of Sweet Valley High would strike a blow to the spirit of this community from which we might never recover," Marianna began.

She addressed the courtroom in a clear, strong voice, arguing eloquently that the Sweet Valley High football team did more for the community than any strip mall or garden ever could. And once she was done with the emotional details, she moved on to her legal arguments, all of which, once again, made perfect sense to Elizabeth. Her speech was just as good as the other lawyers', if not better. Which really irritated Liz. She wanted to not like the woman. She wanted to have no respect for her. But after Marianna West was done, Elizabeth was finding it difficult not to admire her.

"We'll take a brief recess while I retire to my chambers to deliberate," the judge announced.

Everyone rose as the judge left the room, and then Elizabeth saw her father and Marianna walk out to the lobby together. She jumped up and headed for the door to join them. She was dying to ask her dad how he thought the judge was going to rule. And, if she was being honest, she hoped that talking to the two of them might ease her suspicions a little bit.

But when she got out into the hallway, the first thing she saw was her dad's arm wrapped around Marianna's shoulders. Right there, with half the student body and all their colleagues milling around. What on earth was her father thinking?

"Elizabeth!" her father called jovially, noticing her gaping. He brought Marianna over and Elizabeth steeled herself. This was it. She was about to meet her father's maybe-mistress for the first time. "Marianna, this is my daughter Elizabeth. Intrepid reporter."

"It's nice to finally meet you, Liz," Marianna said, offering her hand. "Your dad talks about you nonstop."

Elizabeth reluctantly shook Marianna's hand. "That's nice."

"So, what did you think about our case?" Mr. Wakefield asked. "Marianna did an excellent job, didn't she?" he added proudly.

Elizabeth had to hold back the bile in her throat. He wasn't even trying to mask his feelings. "Yeah. Great."

Marianna looked at Elizabeth quizzically. "Are you all right?"

"Sure. I'm just . . . I'm trying to keep all the details straight for my story," Elizabeth said. "Actually, I think I need to go take some more notes. I'll—"

"Court is now in session!" the bailiff called out.

An interested murmur shot through the crowd.

"Wow. That was fast," Mr. Wakefield said. "Let's get back in there. See you back home, Elizabeth."

"Nice meeting you!" Marianna called over her shoulder.

Elizabeth stood there for a moment, stunned at the casual blow-off.

"Come on, kid. You're gonna miss the big finale," one of the reporters said as he jostled by.

Elizabeth snapped to and quickly returned to her seat. She made a point of watching only the judge as he took his seat and prepared to render his decision. The entire courtroom held its breath.

"When it comes down to it, this was quite an easy decision for me," the judge began. "I've lived in this town my entire life, and I agree with Ms. West. The Sweet Valley High Gladiators are an integral part of this town's character. Not only that, but under the town's bylaws, any lessor is granted a sixty-day grace period in which to renew their lease, and the school board is well within that limit. Therefore, the petitions of George Fowler and Henry Patman are denied. The school's lease will be renewed."

The judge banged his gavel and the courtroom exploded in cheers. Coach Schultz and Principal Cooper shook hands with Marianna and Mr. Wakefield as the football team and other students in attendance started chanting, "SVH! SVH! SVH!"

Elizabeth stood up and applauded with the rest of the SVH student body, elated that the case had turned out the way she'd hoped. It was a perfect moment, really, soured only by the sight of Marianna hugging Elizabeth's father in glee and Todd Wilkins cheering with his friends as if he were the most carefree guy on earth.

• • •

Jessica jogged up the front walk to her house after the impromptu victory party at Cara Walker's house, feeling like everything was finally going her way. The field was going to stay exactly as it was, cheerleading practice would resume the next day, and she could have sworn that Bruce Patman was checking her out during gym class that morning. Maybe she was finally, *finally* snagging his attention.

When she opened the door, the scents of roasting potatoes and her mother's rosemary chicken filled the air. This day just kept getting better and better.

"Hey, Mom!" Jessica called out, bounding into the

dining room, where Mrs. Wakefield had broken out the good china. "What's going on?"

"We're having a real family dinner tonight," her mother said as she placed silverware around the plates. "It's been far too long."

Jessica studied the table with its linen cloth and gleaming place settings. "Okay, but last time I checked there were only five people in this family."

"Oh, your dad's invited Marianna West over," her mother said happily. "Apparently they have some big announcement to make."

Jessica's heart hit the floor as her mother turned and strode back to the kitchen all smiles. Her father was bringing his mistress over for a family dinner? What was wrong with these people? If a guy was going to announce to his family that he was leaving them for some bodacious babe, shouldn't he do it when said babe was far, far away? Or did he want to rub her hotness in his wife's face?

The front door slammed and in walked Steven. "Something smells good," he said, rubbing his hands together. "I guess I picked the right night to invite Tricia over for dinner."

"What?" Jessica blurted out, whirling on him.

"Whoa, Jess. Chill," Steven said. He raised his hands

and backed up a step. "I knew you had a problem with the Martins, but why so violent?"

"I can't believe you people!" Jessica gasped. "You're bringing home the daughter of the town druggie on the same night dad has chosen to parade his little mistress in front of the entire family. It's gonna be a real white-trash evening at the Wakefield house!"

"Jessica, calm down," Steven said, placing his hands on her arms. "I'm going to ignore your completely ignorant stance on Tricia's family for the moment and skip right to the mistress part. What is going on?"

"Mom just told me that dad is bringing Marianna West home for dinner," Jessica said, feeling desperate. "They're going to make some big announcement. What if he's going to tell us he's leaving us, Steven? What if Mom and Dad get divorced?"

"No. Dad would never just spring it on us like that," Steven said, looking a little pale. "He would talk to Mom first, wouldn't he? He wouldn't bring the woman home."

"Yeah, but we never thought Dad would cheat on Mom either," Jessica whispered. "And now . . ."

In the kitchen, Jessica's mom hummed to the radio as she continued to prepare dinner. All Jessica wanted to do was go in there and tell her what was really going on.

"Okay. Maybe we're wrong," Steven said. "Maybe . . . maybe it'll be fine."

"Yeah, maybe," Jessica said, her heart heavy. "So why do I feel like the whole world's about to come to an end?"

• • •

Elizabeth sat perfectly still on the couch in the living room, between her brother and her sister, overcome with a dread she'd never felt before. Per her mother's request, she, Jessica, and Steven had dressed up slightly, and now they were all lined up, prim and proper, feeling as if they were awaiting a formal firing squad. Meanwhile, their mother and father chatted happily with Tricia Martin and Marianna West, sipping white wine as they stood near the bay window. It was all a little too surreal.

"This is insane. Does anyone else feel like they're in the middle of some Machiavellian play?" Liz asked.

"I'm with ya," Steven replied.

"I have no idea what that means, but this sucks," Jessica put in.

"I just can't believe Tricia is going to be here to

witness this," Steven said, wiping a sweaty palm on the arm of the couch. "I really gotta get that girl a cell phone."

Steven had tried all afternoon to get ahold of Tricia, but apparently she'd been out running errands and had come straight from there. Now she and Marianna, looking like a model in her gorgeous ice blue suit, were blabbering away like long-lost friends.

"All right, everyone. I think we've made enough small talk," Mr. Wakefield said suddenly. "I have a serious announcement to make."

Tricia and Marianna fell silent. Elizabeth and Jessica stared daggers at their father. Steven shifted in his seat, looking like he was about to throw up. Meanwhile, Alice Wakefield just stood there smiling expectantly, probably hoping everyone would enjoy her cooking.

"If you'd all raise your glasses," Ned said, turning toward Marianna. None of his children moved, but Alice and Tricia and Marianna did as they were told. "To Marianna West, the newest partner at Jacob, Wakefield, and Finch."

"What!" Marianna exclaimed. "I got it? I got the promotion?"

Elizabeth stared at Jessica.

"No. Freaking. Way," Jessica said under her breath.

"Congratulations, Marianna," Alice said warmly.

"Thank you. Thanks . . . I . . . I had no idea—"

"They told me I could tell you tonight, but they're going to have a formal reception for you tomorrow," Mr. Wakefield said. "Congratulations, Marianna. All your hard work really paid off."

"All *our* hard work." Marianna put down her wineglass and crossed the room to hug Ned. Then she hugged Alice as well. "This is incredible. I . . . I don't know what to say except . . ." She turned to the room. "Thanks, all of you, for letting me borrow your dad, your husband, so often lately. I couldn't have done this without him."

"And now that it's done, you guys can have me back," Mr. Wakefield announced with a laugh.

"Yes. Exactly," Marianna said, beaming. "And thanks for inviting me over and letting me share this moment with all of you. I don't have family out here, so . . . it means a lot."

"To Marianna," Steven said jovially, standing up and grabbing his glass. The color had returned to his cheeks and he was looking elated now.

"To Marianna!" everyone chorused.

Elizabeth turned around and giddily hugged her

sister. "See? I told you there was nothing to worry about," she joked.

"Yeah, yeah," Jessica said, rolling her eyes. "All hail the smart twin."

Elizabeth laughed and got up to celebrate with Marianna and her family. From this moment forward, she was never going to take anything at face value again.

CHAPTER

16

"IT WAS TOTALLY unreal, Enid. You should have seen the looks on their faces," Elizabeth said as she and her friend waited for their food at Casa del Sol after school the next day. Dozens of people from SVH crammed the booths along the walls, and the small restaurant was filled with their animated voices. Casa del Sol was a favorite hangout for the SVH crowd because of its cheap but good Mexican food, its warm south-of-the-border décor, and its incredible views of the ocean. "I thought Mr. Fowler might actually have an emotion for once."

"Good thing he didn't. He might have hurt something," Enid joked. She grabbed a chip from the basket on the counter and crunched into it. "You know, I'm pretty sure he's had Botox."

"No way," Elizabeth said.

"Uh, yeah!" Enid's eyes widened. "I saw him on the news the other night talking about some building he's putting up in L.A., and I swear his mouth and eyes never moved."

Elizabeth laughed. "I wonder what it's like living with a dad like that."

"Please. I bet Lila never sees him," Enid said as their food was placed before them in colorful plastic baskets.

Elizabeth felt a little thump in her chest, thinking about how awful it would be to not have her dad around. Thank goodness all that Marianna West stuff had been a false alarm. She liked her family just the way it was.

Food in hand, Enid turned around to find a table and nearly tripped over herself. "Actually, I think we should take this to go," she said, dropping the baskets back on the counter.

"What? No tables?" Elizabeth asked, glancing around. Her eyes immediately fell on the sight that had tripped up Enid. Todd Wilkins and Emily Mayer were sitting at a booth near the door, sharing a tray of chips and salsa. Elizabeth felt dizzy. She turned her back to the door so that Todd wouldn't notice her pallor.

Enid put her hand on Liz's back. "Are you okay?"

"Yeah. I'm totally fine," Liz said. "It's no big deal." She smiled at the girl behind the counter. "I'm sorry, would you mind bagging this up? We're going to take it home."

"No problem," the girl replied.

"Don't worry about it, Liz. They're probably just doing a project together. Or waiting for some other people!" Enid suggested hopefully. "I'm sure they're not, like, *together.*"

"I couldn't care less if they're together," Elizabeth said, squaring her shoulders. "I'm so over Todd it's not even funny."

Enid snorted a laugh. "Yeah, right."

"Enid!"

"What? I'm just saying. No one gets over a crush that huge that fast," Enid said.

"Well, I do," Elizabeth protested.

Out of the corner of her eye, she glanced toward Todd's table again. He was laughing at something Emily had just said, his brown eyes dancing. Elizabeth's heart deflated like a helium balloon someone had just sucked all the air out of. She clenched her teeth and gave herself an inner smack. It was not supposed to hurt to see that jerk flirting with another girl. If she should have been worried about anything, it was Emily. The girl had no idea what she was getting into.

Elizabeth stood there, growing increasingly tense every time Todd laughed or spoke. Enid yammered on about some MTV show she'd watched the night before, trying to distract her, but it didn't remotely work. Finally, their bags of food were ready and Elizabeth snatched hers up with a quick "Thanks."

"Let's go," she said to Enid. Head held high, she started for the door. At first she intended to ignore Todd and Emily's presence, but then she realized that would be rude. Emily was her friend, and she'd done nothing wrong. The bigger person would stop and say hello—show Todd that she was so unaffected by this that she'd even talk to his date.

"Hi, Emily!" Liz said brightly, pausing by the table.

"Hey, guys," Emily replied. "Want to join us?"

"No, that's fine. We're going back to my house to hang out by the pool," Liz said. "But thanks for the offer."

Emily gave her a quizzical look, and Liz suddenly wondered if her voice was maybe sounding a little too shrill. "Okay."

"Hi, Liz," Todd said. "Enid."

"H-hi Todd," Enid said, looking at Elizabeth uncertainly.

Elizabeth simply shot him a narrow-eyed look before turning around and striding right out the door. Enid was so stunned she had to jog to catch up.

"Liz! What was that?" she asked.

"I cannot believe he really expects me to talk to him after everything he's done." Elizabeth was fuming.

"Okay, I'm starting to think there's something you're not telling me here," Enid said, walking around to the driver's side of her car.

Elizabeth stopped on the other side and took a deep breath. She hadn't told anyone what Todd had done to Jessica, but she was starting to feel as if she had to let it out. And she knew she could trust Enid not to gab about it to the entire school.

She yanked open the car door and tossed her food inside. "I'll tell you on the way."

CHAPTER 17

"I AM *SO* loving this piña colada!" Cara announced, sliding into a booth at Casa del Sol on Saturday night.

"They served you a piña colada?" Elizabeth asked, shocked. Casa had a liquor license, but they were very strict about not serving to underaged kids.

"No! It's virgin," Cara said, rolling her eyes.

"We all know you're a virgin, Cara. You don't need to announce it to the world," Jessica joked, dropping down next to her.

"Ha ha," Cara said.

Enid slid into the seat next to Elizabeth's and distributed

their food from the tray. Liz sat back and sighed, glad her crazy week was finally over.

"This was a good idea," she said, reaching for the hot sauce. "Girls' night out!"

"Please. It's pathetic," Jessica replied. "It's Saturday night. We should be out with the guys!"

"Which guys, exactly?" Cara asked, raising her eyebrows as she sipped her icy drink.

"I don't know. Just . . . guys," Jessica said.

"That's our Jessica. As long as it has testosterone and is breathing, she's in," Cara said, earning a laugh from Liz and Enid. Elizabeth saw her sister shoot Enid an annoyed look, as if she had made the joke rather than just laughed at it.

Just then, the doors opened, and as if Jessica had conjured them, a big group of guys in Sweet Valley High varsity jackets walked in. Ken Matthews was among them, as was, Elizabeth was sorry to see, Todd Wilkins. As if he sensed her there, his eyes met hers almost instantly, and he caught her looking at him. Elizabeth blushed and quickly looked away.

"Now, that's better," Jessica said with a sly smile. "I think I'll go over there and help the guys decide what to order."

"You're going over there?" Enid asked, speaking up for the first time all night.

Jessica paused halfway out of the booth and fell back into her seat. "Sorry, Sister Enid, do you disapprove of guys now?"

Enid flushed slightly. "No. I guess I'm just surprised. I mean, if I were you I wouldn't want to be anywhere near—"

Elizabeth held her breath as Enid glanced over at Todd. Jessica followed Enid's gaze, then ever so slowly looked back at Elizabeth. The fury was evident in Jessica's eyes.

"You *told* her?" she screamed.

Elizabeth leaned forward. "Jess, I just—"

"I cannot believe you *told* her!" Jessica said loudly, causing a few people to turn and stare. "That was a secret, Liz! God! I'm your sister! Does that even matter to you anymore?"

"Uh, what the heck are we talking about here?" Cara asked, confused. Enid, meanwhile, sank lower in her seat.

"You know what, forget it!" Jessica said, grabbing her purse. "I'm outta here."

She stormed out, right past the guys, who were clearly amused by the whole spectacle.

"Liz, I'm so sorry," Enid said. "I didn't mean to–"

"It's okay, Enid, just let me out," Elizabeth said, taking her purse as well.

Enid slid out quickly and Elizabeth followed Jessica. Someone who sounded a lot like Todd called after her, asking if everything was okay, but Elizabeth ignored him. Her heart pounded a mile a minute as she jogged across the jam-packed parking lot to her Jeep. She hadn't intended for Jessica to find out she'd told Enid, but she also never would have expected a reaction like that. It wasn't as though Jessica had done anything wrong. She was the victim here.

But then again, Jess hates to be the victim, Elizabeth thought.

"Jess!" she shouted, arriving at the driver's-side door. The seat was empty. "Jess?"

"I'm back here." Jessica raised her arm. She was lying across the backseat of the Jeep, her legs bent, one arm slung over her eyes. "Go away."

"What are you doing back there?" Elizabeth asked.

"I don't have the keys," Jessica grumbled.

"Then how did you get in?"

"We left it unlocked."

"Jessica–"

Her sister turned onto her side, away from Elizabeth.

Liz rolled her eyes and walked around to the passenger side of the car, figuring she could at least sort of see her sister's face from that side. She got in, slammed the door, and turned around, reaching for Jessica's arm.

"Will you please just look at me?" Liz said. "I'm sorry if you didn't want anyone to know, but Enid's my best friend. I had to talk to someone about it."

"Oh, you had to talk to someone about it," Jessica said, shooting daggers with her eyes. "Why is everything always about you?"

Elizabeth's jaw dropped. She could not believe her sister had just said that. All Liz ever did was make concessions for Jessica. She lent her clothes she never saw again. She helped her with her homework at the expense of her own study time. She let her have the good bedroom, the good chaise by the pool, all the damn hot water she wanted. Liz had even stepped aside when it was clear Jessica liked Todd. And now she was accusing Elizabeth of being selfish?

"You know what, Jessica? I was going to try to convince you to come back inside, but if you want to go home and mope, fine." She yanked the keys out of her bag and held them up. "Here are the keys."

"Hey! It's my lucky night! Two slammin' blondes for the price of one!"

Before Elizabeth could even turn her head, someone was opening the driver's-side door of the Jeep. Jessica shot up in her seat as Rick Andover got in behind the wheel.

"I'll take those," he said, grabbing the keys from Elizabeth.

"Rick! What the hell are you doing?" Jessica demanded.

"I figure I owe you one good run," Rick told her. "Since we never got to race that night."

Elizabeth's blood ran cold as Rick started the Jeep. She could smell the alcohol on his breath, even from a couple of feet away.

"Rick. You're drunk," Elizabeth said, making a grab for the ignition.

Rick batted her arm away, hard. Jessica gasped. "Don't you know you're never supposed to interfere with the driver?" he said. He shoved the car into gear and laughed. Elizabeth knew she should just dive out now, and she would have if she'd been alone. But there was no way Jessica could get out of the backseat in time, and she was not about to leave her sister with this psycho. "Now let's see what this baby can do."

With a screech of the tires, Rick peeled out of the parking space. Jessica screamed as Elizabeth fumbled for her seat belt. "Rick, stop the car and let us out. You can have it, okay? Just let us go," Elizabeth shouted.

"What, and have you miss all the fun?"

He jerked the wheel, spinning out the back tires and taking the twins right by the glass windows of Casa del Sol. Elizabeth saw a few people staring out at them, and the gang of SVH guys still hanging by the door.

"Help!" she shouted out the window as she flew by. "You guys! Help!" For a split second, she saw Todd look up. Saw the sheer terror register on his face. And then she was gone.

"Rick, stop!" Jessica shouted, scooting forward and sticking her head between the two front seats. "Just stop and let us out!"

Rick veered in and out of traffic on the highway, earning honks and shouts from every driver he passed. Elizabeth braced her hands on the door and dashboard. This winding road was dangerous even at a normal speed, and Rick was driving like a maniac.

"Are you crazy?" Elizabeth screamed as a pair of headlights came dangerously close.

"That's it. I'm calling nine-one-one." Jessica lifted her cell phone out of her bag and Rick reached right back, plucked it from her fingers, and tossed it out the window. "Rick!" Jessica screeched. "I swear to God—"

"Shut up!" Rick growled as he swerved around an SUV. "I don't wanna hear another word outta you."

Elizabeth stared at Rick as Jessica shrank back in her seat, petrified.

We're going to die, Elizabeth thought. *I am going to die out here.*

"You girls ready for some *real* fun?" Rick asked, taking a sudden turn onto an exit.

"Where are we going?" Elizabeth managed to ask.

"We're gonna go hang out at *my* favorite place," Rick said, his eyes dark. "It might not be as cutesy as Casa del Sol, but I think you're gonna like it."

He turned onto a dark gravel road and wound his way down a steep incline to a dirt parking lot. There were only a few beat up cars and at least a dozen motorcycles. The building was squat and squalid, with neon beer signs in the few windows.

"Kelly's?" Jessica asked tremulously.

Elizabeth swallowed hard. She'd only ever heard of this place. It was a bar that was featured in the local news every other week for fights and code violations. How it was still in business she had no idea.

"Rick, they're never gonna let us into a bar," Elizabeth said, grasping at straws.

Rick cackled. "Kelly's'll let anybody in. Especially if it's a hot girl."

He got out of the car and walked around the front.

"Liz. What're we gonna do?" Jessica said.

Outside there was a flash of headlights as another car pulled down the winding drive. Elizabeth briefly thought of yelling out for help when whoever it was got out of the car, but she figured that anyone going to Kelly's wouldn't be the type of person who would come to their aid.

"I still have my phone. I'll just have to try to get a second alone once we get inside," Elizabeth said quickly.

Rick yanked open Liz's door and her heart flew into her throat. "Well, Elizabeth Wakefield," he said with a leer. "I've already had your sister. Let's see what *you* taste like."

At that moment, a hand came down on Rick's shoulder. He spun around and Elizabeth caught a quick glimpse of Todd Wilkins's face right before his fist met Rick's jaw.

"Todd!" Elizabeth and Jessica both shouted.

Todd backed up, ready to fight, as Rick righted himself. "That was a big mistake," Rick said.

"You've got one chance to walk away," Todd said, clenching his jaw. His eyes smoldered with fury. "The rest of my friends are about two minutes behind me."

"Can't handle things on your own, superstar?" Rick taunted. "That's fine. It means we've got two minutes to party."

He threw a punch across Todd's face, and Elizabeth winced as Todd's head whipped back. Blood trickled from his lip, but he didn't hesitate. He rushed Rick and tackled him right into the side of his car with a slam.

"Omigod!" Jessica cried, covering her face.

Rick had the wind knocked out of him, and Todd took the split second to bring his fist down one more time across Rick's cheek. That was all it took. Rick slumped to the ground near the wheel of Todd's car, out cold. Apparently, it wasn't so easy to fight back when he was trashed.

Chest heaving, Todd walked over to the Jeep. "Are you okay?"

Elizabeth stepped out, trembling from head to toe. All she wanted to do was hug him. She wanted to throw herself into his arms and cry. She wanted to thank him. But she held back. This was still Todd. She had no idea *what* to feel toward him.

"We're fine," she said finally. "But you're . . . you're bleeding."

Todd brought the back of his hand to his mouth and looked at the stain. "It's nothing."

He stepped toward her, and the air between them seemed to thin. Elizabeth couldn't breathe. He wanted to hold her too. She could practically feel the heat coming off his skin. Maybe if she just—

"Oh, Todd! I can't believe you did that!" Jessica cried, rushing forward and throwing her arms around his neck. "I thought he was going to kill us out here. I really did! Did you follow us all the way from Casa? Omigod, I could *kiss* you."

The entire time Jessica was rambling and pressing herself against him, Todd never took his eyes off Elizabeth. She stepped closer to him, all logic gone from her mind. Todd unwrapped Jessica's arms from his neck. He put his hands on her waist and moved her aside.

"Not this time, Jessica," Elizabeth heard herself say. "This one's mine."

Then, with the briefest of smiles, Todd pulled Elizabeth to him, and their lips met for the very first time.

● ● ●

"I can't believe you kissed Todd," Jessica ranted as Elizabeth drove them, very slowly and carefully, back to their house. "I can't believe you kissed him right there in front of me."

"I can't believe *you* were going to kiss him after every-thing he supposedly did to you," Elizabeth replied. She glanced in the rearview mirror at Todd's car, a few lengths behind theirs. He had insisted on following them home to make sure they were all right, while Ken and the rest of the team waited back at Kelly's for the police to arrive.

"Supposedly? Oh, it's supposedly now. One kiss and you're doubting me," Jessica said.

Elizabeth pulled into their driveway and killed the engine. "I hate to say it, Jess, but I've been sort of wondering about it all along. Did it really happen the way you told me it did that night?"

Jessica gaped at Elizabeth. "How can you even ask me that? You saw how upset I was!"

"Yeah, and I also know what a good actress you are," Elizabeth said. "What I don't know is *why* you would lie about something like that."

Jessica gasped. "I did not lie!"

Behind them, Todd got out of the car. Elizabeth heard the pop of his door and saw him walking toward them in the side mirror. "Well, here's Todd right now. Why don't we just ask him about it? Get it all out in the open?"

Jessica's face went ashen and she quickly opened her door. "I don't think I'm up to that right now, Liz. I mean, we were practically just killed. I'm just going to go inside and get to bed."

Elizabeth smirked. So it was true. Jessica had made the whole thing up. Normally she would be furious with her sister, but right then she was still flying from her kiss with Todd and anticipating another. She knew it was in her best interest to just let her sister go . . . for now.

"Fine. Later, Jess."

"Later!" Jessica waved a hand as she hightailed it for the front door.

Meanwhile, Todd arrived at Elizabeth's window. "Hey."

His voice sent pleasant shivers all through her body. "Hey."

He opened the door for her and she stepped out just as shakily as she had at Kelly's, though now for different reasons. Good reasons. Todd hadn't done a thing to Jessica. He was here. He had kissed her. And from the look on his face, he was ready to do it again.

"So. We have some stuff to talk about," Elizabeth said.

Todd sighed and looked at the ground. "It wasn't you, was it? That first time with Rick. It was Jessica."

"Finally believe me?" Liz said.

"I heard what Rick said to you back there. About having . . . *had* Jessica—"

"He didn't *have* her," Elizabeth said. "Not like that. I think they just kissed."

Todd chuckled. "Still defending her."

"It's a knee-jerk reaction," Elizabeth said with a smile.

"So when she told me it was really her out there, she was telling the truth."

"Yep."

Although it might have been the only truth she's told in the past month.

"God, I'm such a moron," Todd said, leaning back against the Jeep and tilting his chin toward the sky. "I should have known. I mean, I know you. I should have known you would never go out with Rick Andover."

"It's not like you're the only one who believed it," Elizabeth said, leaning next to him. "Don't feel so bad."

"I can't believe *you're* trying to make *me* feel better."

"Well, let's just say I was guilty of the same thing. I believed something about you that I should have known wasn't true."

"What?" Todd asked.

"Trust me, you don't want to know," Elizabeth replied.

Todd looked her in the eye. "I should have just asked you to the dance in the beginning. I should have just sucked it up and asked you."

Elizabeth's heart expanded in her chest. "Why didn't you?"

"I figured you already had a date," Todd said. "Jessica was always talking about how popular you are. How all these guys wanted to take you, and—"

Elizabeth cracked up laughing. "Man, she really covered her bases, didn't she?"

"Who did?"

"Jessica," Elizabeth said. She was going to have to kill that girl later. Or maybe cut off all her hair. Do something as immature as what Jessica had done. But for now, she didn't want to think about her sister. She reached for Todd's hand and he turned toward her. "Want to make a pact?"

"Sure," Todd said with a playful smile.

"Let's each promise never to believe anything Jessica says about the other ever again," Elizabeth said.

Todd laughed lightly. "Sounds like a plan." He stepped even closer to her, so close their knees touched. "Should we kiss on it?"

"Sounds like a plan," Elizabeth said breathlessly.

She tipped her face to his and Todd kissed her lips

gently. Then he slipped his arms around her waist and pulled her close, kissing her more deeply than she'd ever been kissed before. By the time he broke away again, Elizabeth was out of breath and floating somewhere overhead.

"I've been wanting to do that since the first day of school," Todd said in her ear. "You were the only one I ever wanted, Liz."

Elizabeth's very toes tingled. "You have no idea how good that is to hear."

CHAPTER
18

ELIZABETH FLOATED THROUGH the house and up the stairs to her bedroom. She closed the door behind her and leaned against it, taking a deep breath as she replayed Todd's kiss in her mind. She could still feel his lips on hers, his arms around her. The reality had been a hundred times better than any of her daydreams.

Thanks to Rick Andover, this could have been the worst night of Elizabeth's life. But thanks to Todd, it had been the best.

The door that connected Jessica's room to their shared bathroom opened, and Liz could hear Jessica rooting around in her makeup drawer. She narrowed her eyes and sauntered over to the open door on her side. This was going to be interesting.

"Jessica?"

Her sister looked up and smiled. "Oh. Hey, Liz. I'm just looking for that new eyeliner I bought. Have you seen it?"

"That's not going to work," Liz said, crossing her arms over her chest.

"What's not going to work. The eyeliner?" Jessica said with wide-eyed innocence. "It better. I just got it last weekend."

She turned around and walked back into her own bedroom. Elizabeth quickly followed. "No, I'm talking about your diversion tactics. They're not going to work."

"Liz, could you speak in English, please?"

"Your plan backfired, Jess," Elizabeth informed her sister. "Todd just asked me out. We're together now. No thanks to you."

Jessica turned around from her vanity table. "That's great, Liz. I'm very happy for you."

"Will you just quit the innocent act already, Jess? I know what you did!" Elizabeth said. "I know you lied to Todd about me being oh so popular with the guys. I know you lied to me about him attacking you. And you let him believe you were just being protective of me when you told him it was you out on Coast Road with Rick. You have done everything you could possibly think of to keep me away from him and all I want to know is *why*?"

Jessica stared at Elizabeth as if she really were speaking a foreign language. "Liz, I don't know what you're talking about. I never would have—"

"Don't lie to me, Jess!" Elizabeth shouted, clenching her fists. Jessica flinched, and for once Elizabeth was sure she had her undivided attention. "Have you not seen how miserable I've been for the past month? You're not an idiot, Jessica. You must have known I liked him. And from what Todd just told me, you knew he liked me too. How could you do this to me?"

Jessica's face was like stone. "Wow. You really hate me, don't you?"

"No, I don't hate you. But this is probably the closest I've ever come to it," Elizabeth replied. "How could you do this, Jess? Why? Did you really like Todd that much?"

"Well, yeah, I mean . . . I liked him . . . ," Jessica said, walking over to her bed.

"Did you like him, or did you just not want me to have him?" Elizabeth asked.

Jessica's shoulders slumped slightly. Suddenly, she looked five years younger. Like she had when she was a little girl being scolded by their parents. "I don't know," she admitted quietly.

Elizabeth stood over her. She wasn't sure whether she wanted to smack her sister or hug her. But her anger deflated slightly. At least Jessica wasn't lying to her anymore. "Wow. An honest answer." She sat down on the bed next to Jessica. "If you weren't even sure you really liked him, then why go to all that trouble?"

"I don't know, Liz. I swear. I don't know why I do this stuff sometimes," Jessica said, eyeing Elizabeth desperately. "I guess I was jealous or . . . I don't know. Sometimes things just come out of my mouth without me even thinking about them."

"So you're telling me that all of this just happened? You didn't plan any of it?" Elizabeth said.

Jessica looked away. "Well, not *all* of it . . ."

Elizabeth snorted a laugh. Her sister was out of her mind.

"You're laughing?" Jessica asked, astonished.

"Don't get the wrong idea. I'm still mad," Elizabeth

said. "I just . . . I guess I'm less mad because it all worked out in the end."

"Omigod, I know! I saw the way he kissed you out there in the driveway," Jessica said. "He never kissed me like that, Liz. I mean, that was—"

Elizabeth held up a hand. "Let's just pretend from now on that he never actually kissed you at all, okay?"

Jessica shrugged. "Sure. If that's what you want. But wouldn't that sort of be lying? And you've made it pretty clear how much you hate lying," she teased.

Elizabeth shook her head. "You know what's so great about you, Jess? You're always *you*."

"Thanks!" Jessica said happily. "Does that mean you forgive me?"

"It means I'm going to bed now," Elizabeth said.

Jessica reached over and hugged her. Elizabeth stiffened for a moment, but then hugged her back. It was one of her major weaknesses. She could never stay mad at her twin for long.

"I'm really happy for you, Liz. You and Todd were, like, made for each other."

Her sincere tone sent a pang through Elizabeth's heart. "Thanks, Jess."

Elizabeth got up and walked to the bathroom, but she

paused at the door to watch as her sister went back to her eyeliner search. Jessica might have thought this was over—that she had wheedled her way out of trouble for the millionth time—but Elizabeth wasn't going to let her off so easy. Jessica might have been the master manipulator, but as of this moment, Elizabeth was determined to get a little revenge of her own.

CHAPTER 19

"HEY, LIZ! CAN I borrow those diamond earrings you bought last summer?" Jessica asked, bouncing into Elizabeth's room in her new light blue cotton dress. She was having one of those nights when she looked good and knew it. All she needed were the perfect accessories to top off her outfit and tonight would be her night. It had to be. There was no way she could let Liz be the only Wakefield twin with a boyfriend for long. She did have her pride.

"Sure, Jess. Here you go."

Elizabeth plucked the earrings out of her jewelry box

and turned around. Her hand whacked into a full cup of soda she had on top of her dresser, and before Jessica could even react, she was drenched.

"Elizabeth!" Jessica cried, her arms out at her sides as soda dripped down her dress. "What's the matter with you?"

"Omigod, Jess! I'm so sorry!" Elizabeth said, covering her mouth with her hands. "Here. Take it off. We'll just throw it in the laundry."

"There's no time to wash it!" Jessica wailed. She untied the wrap waist and stepped out of the dress. She grabbed a tissue from the box on Liz's dresser and dabbed at her skin. "What am I going to wear to the concert?"

"Why don't you wear my new red top?" Elizabeth suggested, diving into her closet. "And that skirt I got at J.Crew? You love that skirt."

Jessica blinked. She had asked Elizabeth to borrow that skirt four hundred times and Liz always said no. And the one time she had snuck in here to steal it, she hadn't been able to find it anywhere.

"Are you serious?" she asked.

"Yeah. It's the least I can do," Elizabeth said, holding the outfit out to her. "Since I killed your dress."

Jessica looked down at the rumpled mess on the

floor. "True. It *is* the least you can do." She took the hangers and started for her room. "Could you throw that in the washing machine for me? I don't want it to stain."

"You got it," Liz said with a grin.

"What are you smiling about?" Jessica asked.

"Nothing." Elizabeth shrugged. "I'm just psyched for tonight. Big concert celebrating our victory over the Patmans and Fowlers. It's gonna be fun."

Jessica rolled her eyes. "You're just excited because you get to go with Todd."

"Maybe." Liz preened.

"Make me barf."

Jessica went back to her room to change and pick out the right shoes for the outfit. She fastened Elizabeth's earrings in her ears and clipped her hair up on one side so people could see and admire them. Last summer Elizabeth had saved all her money from her part-time job to pay for them, missing out on several nights at Casa and wearing all the same old T-shirts from the year before. Jessica had not understood it at the time—she'd blown all her cash as soon as she'd gotten her hands on it—but now she wondered if Liz had been right all along. These earrings were gorgeous. Of course, as long as Jessica lived with responsible Liz, she'd have access to all the nice things Elizabeth saved up for. It was a win-win situation, really.

"Okay. I'm ready," Jessica said, returning to Elizabeth's room. Liz was just checking herself out in the mirror. She was wearing a black sundress Jessica had never seen before and had her hair down around her shoulders. "Wow. You look hot."

"Thanks," Elizabeth said. "First real date with Todd and all. I felt like dressing up."

Jessica stepped up next to her sister and eyed their reflections in the mirror. "You know, if I didn't know any better, I'd swear that you were me and I was you," Jessica said with a smile.

Elizabeth frowned thoughtfully. "Huh. You might be right."

A horn honked out on the street and Elizabeth grabbed her purse. "That's Todd! Let's go!"

Jessica grudgingly followed. "I don't know why I agreed to go with you guys. You're going to be slobbering all over each other the whole ride there."

"You agreed because you're hoping to get Bruce Patman to drive you home, remember?" Elizabeth said over her shoulder as she headed down the stairs.

"Oh yeah. That's right!" Jessica was happy again at the

thought of Bruce. So happy she practically skipped down the stairs and out to Todd's car. Tonight could definitely turn out to be a night to remember.

• • •

Todd parked the car all the way in the back of the lot—one of the few spots left. Elizabeth could already hear the pounding beat of the music coming from the newly constructed stage on the far side of the bleachers. Some new band was opening up for Valley of Death, and from what she could tell, that opening act was still on. Their timing couldn't have been more perfect.

"Come on, guys. I don't want to miss Dana's first song," Elizabeth said as they got out of the car.

Elizabeth took Todd's hand and he squeezed it, giving her a conspiratorial smile. Her heart warmed, and it took a lot of self-control to keep from laughing. If her plan went off, this was going to be a very interesting night.

The lights were on over Gladiator Field, and hundreds of students milled around in front of the stage, chatting, cheering for the music, and noshing on snacks from the snack bar. Elizabeth, Todd, and Jessica ducked into the crowd and made their way to the front, greeting a few friends along the way. As soon as they got to the stage, the song came to a close and everyone cheered. Elizabeth scanned the area and saw Dana Larson chatting near the side of the stage with Emily Mayer.

"I'll be right back, you guys. I have to talk to Dana about an article I'm doing on the band for the Oracle," Elizabeth said.

"We'll be fine," Todd told her.

Jessica, however, shot her a panicked look. Liz knew her sister didn't want to be left alone with the guy she had lied to and about so recently. That was why Elizabeth was counting on Todd to keep her there somehow. Otherwise, this thing would be over before it even got off the ground.

Liz's heart pounded as she approached Dana. Up onstage, the other lead singer announced the main event:

"And now, here they are! Valley! Of! Death!"

Dana was just charging up the stairs to the stage when Elizabeth reached out and grabbed her arm. She almost tripped and her eyes narrowed in anger when she saw who was holding on to her.

"Jessica, what are you doing?" she said.

Elizabeth's face turned pink with pleasure. It was working! The plan was already working!

"Sorry, Dana," she said, putting on Jessica's favorite

sickly sweet tone. "But trust me. This, you're gonna want to hear."

"Well, make it fast. My band is already onstage, in case you hadn't noticed."

Elizabeth smiled slyly. "I know who writes the Insider," Elizabeth said. "I just thought *you* might want to make the announcement. But if you don't want to know . . ."

Dana's kohl-rimmed eyes widened. "No! No! I want to know!" she said, all ears now. If there was one thing Dana Larson lived for, it was mayhem of any kind. Especially if she could be an integral part of it.

"It's my sister. Liz writes it."

"No way," Dana said, glancing into the crowd. "Where is she?"

"She's right over there with Todd Wilkins. Where she *always* is," Elizabeth said, pointing. Luckily, Todd had done his job. Jessica was still standing front and center with him, and they even appeared to be getting along.

"Perfect," Dana said, smiling slowly. "This is gonna be good."

Oh, yes, it is, Elizabeth thought.

Dana bounded up onto the stage and took the microphone. Behind her, Emily banged her drumsticks together, counting out the beat for their first song, but Dana held up her hand to stop her.

"Attention, people! Attention! Hey! Shut it!" Dana shouted. The crowd fell silent. "I have an announcement to make that you are *so* gonna thank me for," Dana said. "You all know I'm not big on tradition, but if there's one Sweet Valley High tradition I love, it's the annual dunking of the Insider columnist."

The crowd cheered. Dana wasn't the only one who loved this silly ritual.

"And I just happen to know who's been writing the column this year," Dana said. "Do you want to know who it is?"

"Yeah!" Everyone cheered.

"Oh, please. I said, do you want to know who it is?" Dana shouted.

"Yeah!" They cheered louder.

"Well, good, because she's standing right in front of me, right now!" Dana said, pointing into the crowd. "Elizabeth Wakefield, come and get your dunking!"

Elizabeth watched from afar as Jessica's eyes widened. One of the guys behind her grabbed her under the arms while another picked up her legs by the ankles.

"Omigod! No! Put me down, you idiots! I'm Jessica!" she shouted.

"Nice try, Liz," Dana said into the microphone. "We

may have fallen for that twin-switch crap back in grade school, but we've figured it out by now!"

Elizabeth laughed into her hand as the guys marched right by her with Jessica in their arms, leading pretty much the entire student body to the pool.

"Get off me! I am *not* going in the pool!" Jessica shrieked. She looked around wildly and caught Elizabeth's eye. "Liz! Tell them! Tell them I'm me!"

Elizabeth simply laughed and waved. Todd caught up to her and grabbed her hand as they joined the throng.

"This was the best idea ever," he said happily. "Who knew you were such an evil genius?"

"Take it as a warning. Don't ever mess with Elizabeth Wakefield," she joked as they jogged along.

"I'll remember that," Todd said, giving her a quick kiss.

Liz was flushed with pleasure as the crowd reached the pool. Finally, the guys carrying Jessica got to the edge of the deep end. They swung Jessica between them.

"One!" the whole crowd counted as Jessica swung.

"Stop! No!"

"Two!"

"Oh, you guys suck!" Jessica spat.

"Three!"

With a shriek, Jessica went flying, and the whole crowd went wild. Everyone waited for her to surface, which she did a minute later, shoving her hair out of her face and paddling to the ladder with as much dignity as she could possibly muster. She pulled herself up and out, then stood there, dripping, while everyone applauded.

"Yeah, yeah. Very funny," Jessica said, raising a hand. "You're all going to get yours. I hope you know that."

The crowd started to disperse and Elizabeth and Todd made their way over to Jessica with a towel Todd had asked Winston to bring with him to the concert. Elizabeth held the towel out to her sister.

"You were right, Jess. You really did look like me tonight," Elizabeth said with a triumphant smile.

Jessica gaped at her sister. "You *planned* this?"

"Let's see . . . soda spill? Check. Benevolent offer of J.Crew skirt? Check."

"Convincing her to come with us because Bruce might drive her home later?" Todd suggested.

"Right! Check. Giving Dana Larson my perfect Jessica impression? Check."

"Oh. My. God. Liz, you're pure evil," Jessica said. There was fire in her eyes, but unless Elizabeth was mistaken, there was pride in her voice.

"Well, Jess," Elizabeth said, patting her sister on the shoulder. "I learned from the best."

"Have fun tonight, Jessica," Todd said, then winced as he looked her over. "But don't count on a ride home from Patman. He lives for his leather seats."

He put his arm around Elizabeth and the two of them walked off to enjoy the concert together, leaving Jessica groaning, cursing, and wringing out her clothes.

CHAPTER

1

JESSICA WAKEFIELD SMOOTHED the front of her new Hawaiian-print Roxy dress and held her head high as she strode along the outdoor walkway to her locker at Sweet Valley High. She heard a couple of giggles as she passed by a group of sophomores, but couldn't tell exactly whom they'd come from, so she just shot the whole group a look of death until they all clammed up; then she kept right on walking.

Sooner or later the chatter about what had happened to her last Saturday night was going to die down, and if Jessica had anything to say about it, it would be sooner rather than later.

Her best friends, Cara Walker and Lila Fowler, stood

near the wall up ahead, their heads bent together as they chatted happily. Friendly faces. Thank God.

"Hey, guys!" Jessica called out, grabbing her lock.

Cara instantly closed her cell phone and shoved it behind her back, looking guilty.

"What was that?" Jessica asked suspiciously.

"Oh, nothing," Cara said. She turned to her own locker mirror to check her long, dark hair. Then she glanced sidelong at Lila and they both cracked up.

"You haven't deleted the pictures yet, have you," Jessica accused Cara, whipping open her locker. "Cara! You promised me you'd get rid of them!"

"We're sorry, Jess, but come on," Lila said, taking Cara's phone out of her hand. "These are hilarious."

She held out the phone with her perfectly manicured fingers, as if Jessica really wanted to see how Cara had caught the worst moment of her life on her camera phone. She glanced over, thinking maybe it hadn't been as bad as she recalled, and there she was, pulling herself out of the Sweet Valley High School pool, fully clothed, with black mascara running down her face. In the background, a couple of kids laughed as if they were about to bust something. Nope. It was just as bad as she remembered.

"I swear, if that little stunt Elizabeth pulled keeps me from getting nominated for homecoming queen, I am going to take pictures of her in the shower and post them on her precious little blog," Jessica ranted, shoving a couple of books into her locker and closing it with a bang.

"God, Jess. Take a joke," Lila said, rolling her big brown eyes. She fished in her Louis Vuitton backpack for a pot of lip gloss and nudged Cara aside so that she could see her reflection while she applied. "Besides, half the school still thinks it was Liz who got dunked, not you. There's no way you don't make homecoming court."

Jessica sighed and looked in her locker mirror. Her shoulder-length blond hair looked perfect, not a strand out of place, and her new blue eyeliner really brought out her stunning Pacific blue eyes. The gold lavaliere necklace she always wore—a present from her parents on her sixteenth birthday—fell just above the neckline of her new dress. She looked perfect today, she knew. But homecoming court votes were already in. Looking perfect *today* wouldn't help her.

"You know, technically, we should still dump Liz in the pool," Cara pointed out, her green eyes thoughtful. "The tradition is that the Insider columnist gets dunked, right? Well, *Liz* is the Insider columnist, but she made us all believe you were her so that you would get dunked. Ergo, she needs to get wet."

Jessica smirked. "I like the way you think, Cara Walker."

"Since when do you say 'ergo'?" Lila asked, a tiny wrinkle in her otherwise beautiful tan brow.

"Since I started taking that SAT course," Cara responded with a sniff.

"Attention, students!" Principal Cooper's voice suddenly boomed over the PA system. "We have your results for this year's homecoming court."

"Omigod! This is it!" Jessica gasped, grabbing Lila's and Cara's arms. A sizzle of anticipation raced through the warm California air. Most of the people in the outdoor hallway stopped gabbing so they could hear. Jessica held her breath.

"First, your candidates for homecoming king," the principal announced. There was a shuffling of papers and he cleared his throat. "They are . . . Winston Egbert."

"What?" Jessica cried, causing Lila and Cara to laugh. "Is this the joke court?" Winston was basically the biggest dork in school. Jessica had always thought he looked just like that Waldo guy from the *Where's Waldo?* books.

"Ken Matthews," the principal continued.

"Okay, well at least *that* makes sense," Jessica added as Ken, the gorgeous blond captain of the football team, accepted congratulations from his friends down the hall.

"Bruce Patman."

Yes! Jessica cheered silently. She'd had a crush on Bruce ever since she'd known what the word "crush" meant, and she'd been counting on his making the homecoming court.

"And Todd Wilkins," the principal finished.

"Shocker," Lila said, rolling her eyes.

Of course Elizabeth's perfect boyfriend would make it. If he didn't, he might be less than perfect.

"And now your candidates for homecoming queen," Principal Cooper continued. "Lila Fowler."

Lila preened, flicking her light brown hair over her shoulder and running a fingertip along one plucked eyebrow. The people around her applauded, and Jessica smiled, even though inside she was burning with jealousy and dread. Jealousy that Lila always got everything, dread that her own name might not also be on the list.

"Enid Rollins."

"Okay. Now I *know* this is a joke," Jessica said.

"Hey!" Lila protested, whacking her with the back of her hand.

"What? I mean, Enid? Come on. She might be an even bigger loser than Winston," Jessica said.

"And she's your sister's best friend," Lila pointed out. "So what does that make Liz?"

Jessica shot Lila a silencing look. Jessica could bad-mouth her twin as much as she wanted, but she didn't like it when other people tried to do the same.

"You get one hot boyfriend and all of a sudden you're

homecoming court material," Cara said with a sigh, leaning back against the wall.

"You think that's why? Because she's going out with Ronnie Edwards?" Jessica asked, incredulous.

"Well, he's new. He's hot. He's all mysterious and brooding," Cara said with a shrug. "When she snagged him it totally upped her It factor."

Jessica pondered this. She'd never quite thought of Ronnie Edwards as mysterious and brooding—more silent and robotic—but she could see how some girls might find him attractive. Maybe Cara was on to something.

"Elizabeth Wakefield," the principal continued.

Oh please, please, please let the last name be mine! Jessica begged the popularity gods.

"And Jessica Wakefield," he finished.

"Yes!" Jessica shouted, jumping up and down.

Cara laughed, but Lila shot her a look of disdain. "Very sophisticated, Jess. Not at all embarrassing."

Jessica composed herself and accepted congratulations from Ken and his friends as they passed by. Then she saw Bruce himself come around the corner, and it was as if everything just switched into slow motion. He walked down the center of the hall as though he owned the place, his dark hair shiny in the sun, that perpetual smirk in his brown eyes. He was wearing a pristine blue Ralph Lauren sweater and distressed jeans, and looked like he could sail off on his yacht at any second. Which, of course, with his family's money, he could probably do. Jessica watched him until he strolled by, hoping for that rare and coveted hello.

"Ladies," he said with a brief nod.

Jessica almost melted.

"Wow, Jess. You look like you just saw your first Roberto Cavalli," Lila commented snidely. "Try rolling your tongue back into your mouth."

Cara snorted a laugh that brought Jessica back to earth.

"I don't care what you think, Lila," Jessica said, tossing her hair back. She gave herself a confident, steadying look in the mirror, hoping her crazy heartbeat would chill out before she overheated. "Bruce Patman is going to be mine eventually. And now that we're in homecoming court together, I'm that much closer."

Excerpt copyright © 2008 by Francine Pascal
Published by Laurel-Leaf Books
an imprint of Random House Children's Books
a division of Random House, Inc.
New York
Originally published by Bantam Books in 1983.